One on One

ALSO BY ANDREA MONTALBANO

Out of Bounds
Caught Offside

One on One

Andrea Montalbano

sourcebooks
jabberwocky

Published by Sourcebooks Jabberwocky, an imprint of Sourcebooks, Inc.
P.O. Box 4410, Naperville, Illinois 60567-4410
(630) 961-3900
Fax: (630) 961-2168
sourcebooks.com

Library of Congress Cataloging-in-Publication Data

Names: Montalbano, Andrea, author.
Title: One on one / Andrea Montalbano.
Description: Naperville, Illinois : Sourcebooks Jabberwocky, [2018] | Series:
   Soccer Sisters ; 3 | Summary: At soccer camp, Soccer Sisters Makena and
   Val not only help Chloe build her self-confidence on the field, they also
   help her cope with archrival Skylar Wilson's bullying.
Identifiers: LCCN 2017034430 | (13 : alk. paper)
Subjects: | CYAC: Soccer--Fiction. | Camps--Fiction. | Teamwork
   (Sports)--Fiction. | Friendship--Fiction. | Bullying--Fiction. |
   Self-confidence--Fiction.
Classification: LCC PZ7.M76342 One 2018 | DDC [Fic]--dc23 LC record available at
https://lccn.loc.gov/2017034430

Source of Production: Berryville Graphics, Inc. Berryville, Virginia, USA
Date of Production: February 2018
Run Number: 5011527

Printed and bound in the United States of America.
BVG 10 9 8 7 6 5 4 3 2 1

To my soccer sisters: Brandi Chastain, Stacey Vollman Warwick, and Marian Smith. I'm never one on one with you on my team.

C hloe Gordon considered thirteen a decent amount of years. Take the word *thirteen*, for example. It's got *teen* right there in it, and teens are definitely not kids anymore.

Try telling that to her parents.

"Did you pack that sunscreen I got you from the dermatologist?" Chloe's mother, Jenna, called from her room. "And your blankie?"

"My *blankie*?" Chloe muttered under her breath. Her mom had to be kidding.

With a sigh, Chloe finished zipping up her toiletry bag filled with ponytail holders, acne cream, and—just in case—a few emergency girl supplies.

"Yes, *Mommy*," Chloe finally answered in a risky tone, "I packed it all. And my blan*ket*."

Chloe was less annoyed with her meddling mother

than she sounded. (And truth be told, she did have a special blanket she always slept with.) Chloe was actually kind of amused her mother was "helping" her pack at all. Jenna Gordon was not exactly what you would call hands-on. Chloe couldn't recall a single time that anyone other than her nanny, Ana, had ever helped her pack for a trip.

Then again, Chloe had never gone on a trip like this before.

She was packing for two weeks at World Cup Soccer Camp with her Soccer Sisters, Makena and Val. Chloe had been looking forward to the trip for months. It had been all she and the girls talked about. But as thrilled and excited as she was, she knew her parents could not have been less happy if she'd shaved her head and tattooed her ears. *Maybe that's next*, Chloe thought. As a reflex, she ran her hand down her long, blond, perfect fishtail braid and chuckled. Maybe not.

Chloe took a last look at the packing list. Cleats, indoor shoes, shin guards, ball, water bottles, sweats, shirts, shorts, sheets. A book. That was it. Well, what else did you need for soccer camp?

"I'm ready!" she called. "Dad, can you come help me with my bags, please?"

Chloe listened for a response. Nada. This was hardly a

surprise. It invariably took a few tries to get Jack Gordon's attention, and doing so was definitely something Chloe had yet to master in her thirteen long years. She went to look for him, expecting to find her dad in his standard state: on a conference call, glued to one of his countless electronic devices, typing, talking, clicking, or swiping. He texted more often than Chloe, her brother, and all her so-called smartphone-obsessed friends put together.

That's because Jack Gordon worked on Wall Street. To him, his job was excuse enough to be completely oblivious to everything except whatever financial deal or crisis was on his plate. The good news was that he basically never gave Chloe a hard time about texting her buddies.

"Dad!" She raised her voice this time. "We gotta go!" Chloe tugged at her giant duffel. Two weeks' worth of soccer jerseys weighed a *lot*. Next to her duffel sat a smaller suitcase. This was one of her mother's fancy cases, with wheels and some designer logo plastered all over it.

Scowling, Chloe pushed it with her foot. It rolled as smoothly as a roller coaster on a decline. Inside was ten days' worth of leotards and ballet slippers. Ugh. She didn't want to go to ballet camp, but that was the deal she'd made with her parents. If they let her go to soccer camp, she would attend an elite dance training session on some island in the middle of a lake in the Adirondack Park in upstate New York.

With a flounce, Chloe took off to find her father. In truth, the Gordon home was ridiculously huge—way too big for four people. There was a good chance he was three floors away and couldn't hear her even if he wanted to. She trotted down the first flight of carpeted stairs, which were perfect in a contemporary, cold kind of way. The entire house was like that. Jenna Gordon was an interior designer. Chloe was amazed at the amount of time her mother could spend agonizing over something as minor (and ridiculous) as a light bulb or the placement of a flower vase.

"Come on now, I really need to send this email," Chloe heard her father say as she approached his office door. *Typical,* she thought. But who was he talking to?

Outside, she could see her brother, Andrew, throwing a lacrosse ball off a rebounder. Her mother was still upstairs.

Chloe hesitated for a moment and then knocked on the door. She heard her father sigh loudly.

"Yes?" he asked in what sounded like an exasperated tone.

"I'm all packed, Dad," Chloe said from outside the heavy oak door. "Can you help me get the bags downstairs and take me over to Makena's house?"

Her father sighed again. She thought she heard him mutter, "Get out of here."

Chloe stiffened. She knew how much he and her mother disapproved of her going to camp—and playing soccer in general for that matter. They were convinced she was going to sprain an ankle, break a leg, get a black eye, and/or suffer some other rough-girl outcome. When she was young, Chloe's mother had been a ballerina and a model. She had zero experience with team sports. The thought of her daughter's beautiful legs covered in black-and-blue bruises was almost too much to bear. Chloe's father had played football and did understand a bit more, but not much.

Had he changed his mind about letting her go to camp?

Chloe stood frozen, her hand lifted to knock again. She didn't know what to do. She needed to be over at her friend Makena Walsh's house soon so she could catch her ride to camp. She couldn't walk all the way with her heavy bags. Chloe twirled her braid and waited. Tears threatened to fill her eyes.

"Get down!" Jack Gordon said again, this time with a chuckle. Chloe exhaled with relief. She knew immediately he wasn't talking to her.

Gently, Chloe pushed open the door. Sure enough, there was her father, bobbing his head to the left and right to try to get a good look at a large computer monitor. But to no avail: a black-and-white ball of fluff was meowing and spinning in circles on his keyboard, rubbing up against his face, nibbling on his fingers, and jumping up to nip at his nose.

He finally gave up, sitting back to take off his glasses. To his daughter, he shrugged his shoulders, grinned, and said, "She doesn't like it when I click."

Chloe raised her eyebrows, unsure whether to be jealous or proud.

Victorious, the little cat took one last smug jaunt around the computer, jumped into her father's lap, and curled up for a nap. Chloe shook her head in disbelief. She still found it nearly impossible to believe that her father had been captivated and was clearly being controlled by a tiny six-pound stray kitten.

"I guess she doesn't like it when you work all the time" was all Chloe managed to say, thinking to herself, *I don't like it much either*.

Her dad ignored the comment, if he even heard it. "What's up?" he asked.

"Uh, I was wondering if you could help me with my bags? I need to be at Makena's house soon."

Her father shook his head. "I have a call. Karl will take you over there, and Andrew can help with the bags."

Chloe was disappointed but not surprised. Karl was her parents' driver, and he got Chloe to most of her practices and other events.

She looked at the floor.

Her father stopped typing on his computer. "Chloe, are you sure about this?"

"Of course I am," Chloe said, feeling immediately defensive. "We made a deal, right?"

Chloe's father held up his right hand (the left was too busy petting the kitten) and said, "I know. I know. Two weeks of soccer in exchange for ten days of ballet—and whatever kind of secret sign language stuff your mother wants."

Chloe chuckled. "It's not sign language. Mom wants me to do something like this whenever they take my picture." She gave her father a thumbs-up and a big fake smile. There were two parts to their deal. Chloe could go to soccer camp if, (1) she attended, without complaint, an elite ballet camp for ten days and, (2) she sent photo signals via the camp's daily picture blog. Jenna Gordon had read some *New York Times* article about how to check up on your kids at camp and thought the idea was so clever. All Chloe had to do was remember to look happy and "pretty" for the camera.

How hard could that be?

As if her father was reading her mind, he said, "You seem to have become quite a good negotiator."

"Not as good as that one," Chloe said, laughing. Coming over to pet the little cat, she shook her head in amazement. Never, ever, *ever* had any kind of pet been allowed in the Gordon household before.

But all that had changed—sort of—a month earlier.

Chloe's father had been working late as usual. The temperatures were unseasonably cold for late May in New York, and a damp chill hung in the air. He told Chloe and Andrew that he had heard a small sound as he walked into the parking garage at his office, but he didn't pay it much attention. When he reached his car and opened the door, however, he turned to see a small, wet, cold kitten staring at him. He turned to go, but the little cat gave a tiny, confident meow, flopped on her back, and put her paws in the air.

That was it. Something about the little animal's bravado melted her father's heart. He scooped her up and brought her home to Brookville, the community north of New York City where the Gordons lived. He found some newspaper and a box and installed the kitten next to his bed.

Chloe and Andrew tried to eavesdrop on the

knock-down, drag-out argument when their mother saw the kitten but could only hear muffled "forget its" and "replace anything she destroys" threats. Their dad had prevailed, however, and their mother stormed out in a huff, announcing that her husband was "smitten with the kitten."

So that's what they named her. Smitty the Kitty.

"Mom pet her yet?" Chloe asked her father.

"Are you kidding?" He snorted. "It's a good thing your mother doesn't cook, or we'd be having kitty stew by now."

"Ick," Chloe said.

As if on cue, they both heard Jenna Gordon's footsteps on the stairs.

"Quick, give me that sweatshirt," Chloe's father said. Chloe grabbed the hoodie from a nearby chair and tossed it to him, happy to be partners in crime. He covered the cat and started to read an email just as his wife entered the room.

Chloe didn't bother wiping the grin off her face.

"Well, you look happy to be leaving us," her mother said as she entered.

Chloe took a deep breath. Don't say anything, she willed herself. Just keep your mouth shut for five more minutes, and you're free.

"It's a great camp, Mom. So yeah, I'm excited," Chloe

said in a chirpy voice. She collapsed into a soft, brown leather armchair across from her father's desk. She could see Smitty squirming under the sweatshirt.

"Chloe, you know you don't have to go for the full two weeks. That's a lot of running and…kicking," her mom said.

"I'll be fine. We do get to sleep, you know." Chloe saw her mother raise one perfect eyebrow and knew her tone was wrong.

Jenna Gordon was in her early forties but looked like she was thirty. She was always perfectly coiffed, with sleek hair and just enough makeup to make her glow.

Her mother frowned. "There are lots of things we could go do together, you know. If you stayed. Shopping. A show. Spend the day at a spa…"

Chloe refused to take the bait and said sweetly, "Are you trying to bribe me?"

"No. I'm not. It's just that I can think of a million better ways for you to spend your time."

"Yeah, well, I can't," Chloe said. "There will be coaches from all over the world at camp, watching and playing with us! There's nothing like that for me here."

"Well, it's certainly not going to help your dancing. You know we just want what's best for you. You are a gifted ballerina. And from what I hear, that's not exactly the case with this *soccer*."

Chloe felt a hot flash of anger cross her face. Why couldn't her mother just be proud of her for once? She couldn't hold back. In spite of herself, she stood up and yelled, "I don't care! When are you going to understand? Soccer is *my* sport. It's what *I* love to do. Dancing is what you *make* me do."

Chloe's mother was unmoved. "Chloe, I just don't see the point. If you can't be the best, why bother doing it at all?"

Before Chloe could spit out a response she knew she'd regret, an arm encircled her shoulder. It was Andrew, her older brother. He'd snuck silently into the room.

"Go. Go. Go." He urged in a low, firm voice, shoving her by the elbow. "Zip it. You're so close. Don't blow it now."

A sudden movement broke the glare between mother and daughter. Jack Gordon, grimacing. Oh yes, the claws were out. Jumping up from his chair, he bundled the sweatshirt into a ball and quickly left the room, holding the concealed cat awkwardly in his arms.

"I'll get the bags," he called.

"C an you *believe* her?" Chloe slammed the car door, shouting at the roof above the backseat. For good measure, she kicked the back of the passenger seat. Hard.

"Oi!" Her brother turned around and smacked her in the leg. "Chill. Out."

Chloe growled, "I just do not know where I came from sometimes. Our parents have to be the most clueless human beings on the face of this earth."

"Hey, don't sell them short," Andrew said with a nod. "I'd include Mars, Venus, Jupiter…uh, the entire galaxy, actually."

"True," Chloe said with a laugh and a sigh. If there was one, *and only one*, person in the world she didn't have to explain her parents to, it was Andrew.

"Thanks for coming with me to Makena's," she said as an afterthought.

The ride to Makena's was short, just a few blocks across Brookville, but the camp was more than two hours north. Makena's mother was driving Chloe and Makena and then continuing up to Boston to give some talk on butterfly migration.

"No problem," Andrew said. "That bag is *really* heavy."

Chloe peered into the rearview mirror and saw Karl squinting back at her. He'd known Chloe and Andrew since they were in car seats. He had seen it all, knew it all, and had the amazing ability to communicate with just an eye crinkle, a wink, or the subtle shake of his head.

Karl raised his eyebrows. He and Chloe both knew that even if her duffel bag had been filled with feathers, Andrew would still have felt the need to "help out." That's because Mrs. Walsh was *also* driving Val Flores to camp. Andrew had a massive crush on Chloe's teammate, which had been blossoming since he'd taken her to a dance over the winter. They weren't officially dating or anything, but Andrew never missed a chance to "run into" Val and act like a total lovestruck goofball.

Suddenly thinking of her father, Chloe wondered aloud, "What is the deal with Dad and that kitten?"

"I know, right?" Andrew said, turning around. "Smitty

sleeps in the bed with him now and attacks Mom's toes. Dad thinks it's hysterical. It's like he's having a midlife crisis or something."

"Don't people usually go on a cruise or get a fancy sports car?" Chloe asked.

Andrew raised his hands in the air and shrugged. "Dude, Dad doesn't need any more sports cars." He was right. Their father had a garage full of pricey cars.

Chloe looked out the window, admiring the beautiful homes and manicured lawns as they slipped past. She knew that she lived a privileged life, but luxury didn't mean her family was perfect or happy.

Far from it.

"It's a cat-tastrophe!" she said absentmindedly. "Get it? Cat. Tastrophe."

"I get it, I get it, Hemingway," Andrew said. "Guess that's why you're the one going to camp and I'm the one staying home with a tutor."

"Yeah, that stinks," Chloe said sympathetically. While she was away, Andrew had to have a math and writing tutor. His grades had fallen during the year, and his parents wanted him to make it to High Honors Algebra.

Karl made the last turn onto Makena's block. "We'll have fun while you're away," he said. His first words since they had gotten in the car. Andrew made a fist and offered a bump to Karl.

"That's right, baby. Karl's going to take me to Long Island Sound to do some fishing!"

Karl smiled from the driver's seat.

"You can catch a snack for that kitty cat!" Chloe said with a chuckle.

They pulled up to the house. Makena and Val were already outside. Naturally, they were passing a ball back and forth. Val waved. Chloe wasn't sure who was happier to get out of the car, her or her brother. Not that it mattered. She was sure these were going to be the best two weeks of her life.

Two hours and a hundred miles later, the girls piled out of the Walshes' minivan.

"OMG, this place looks like Hogwarts," Makena said to Chloe as they dragged their bags out of the back of the van.

Chloe agreed, peering up at the beautiful boarding school's ivy-covered walls and stone dormitories.

"Dude, I know!" Val said. "I keep expecting Harry, Ron, and Hermione to come zooming by on their broomsticks."

Chloe stopped and smiled at them both. Thrilled as she was to be attending two weeks of soccer camp, her true joy was hanging out with her Soccer Sisters. Yes, Makena and Val were her teammates, but to Chloe, they were way more than that. They were the kinds of friends who feel like family.

"Girls, I'm going to drop off the paperwork and get

your rooming assignments," Makena's mom said. "Can you wait here with the bags for a minute?"

The girls all shrugged in agreement, and Val grabbed a ball.

"Mac! Think fast!" Val sent a hard pass Makena's way. Though Makena barely had time to react, she still managed to bring the ball gracefully to a stop. Chloe laughed. That was Makena.

Makena, who went by "Mac," lived and breathed soccer. Chloe couldn't remember the last time she hadn't seen her friend wearing a soccer jersey. Tall, and getting taller, with strawberry-blond hair and a sprinkling of freckles, Mac had the heart of a lion. Things on the field changed when she wasn't around. The team's energy fell. Without her, something was missing—something big.

Makena sent a high looping pass to Val. Chloe thought Val was going to trap the ball with her thigh, but at the last second she turned around and basically sat on the ball as it hit the ground and bounced up, hitting her in the rear end.

"Oh, nice butt trap!" Chloe yelled. Val grinned, took a bow, and then began to juggle the ball with ease.

Val Flores was the youngest and smallest girl on their squad, but she was fierce, feisty, and fast. The Breakers liked to call her Val the Bee because she was always buzzing in and could deliver a serious sting. She had black hair so dark it sometimes looked blue, big brown eyes, and a bright smile that contrasted with her cocoa skin. When she grinned, it could light up an entire room. Chloe totally understood why Andrew was such a sucker for Val.

Val passed the ball to Chloe, who flipped it up with her foot and caught it in her hands.

"Nice," Mac said.

Chloe grinned at her friends. "I'm so psyched to be out of Brookville, I cannot tell you," she said. "And to be with you two nuts!"

"Watch this!" Makena launched herself into a cartwheel down a steep hill, which turned out not to be the best idea. She totally wiped out and slid face-first into the grass.

"Blech," she said, spitting out a mouthful of dirt.

Chloe laughed. "Stick to soccer!"

"Oh, here comes my mom," Makena said. "We *better* all be in the same room."

Mrs. Walsh approached, waving a white sheet of paper. The girls got serious. Makena ran over and grabbed the paper out of her mother's hand. She looked at Val and then at Chloe.

She smiled.

Huge grins broke out on Val's and Chloe's faces too.

"We're all together. Grays West. Room 204."

Chloe and Val rushed over to peer at the paper. Sure enough, it confirmed what their parents had requested:

GRAYS WEST/204
V. Flores
C. Gordon
M. Walsh

"Here's the map," Mrs. Walsh said, pointing toward a white-shingled dormitory at the end of a small yard. "That's Grays, right there. I think you guys are in the left-hand side. The other side is Grays East."

Makena's mom hugged all the girls good-bye. Chloe could see she was looking closely at each of them for signs of tears.

"You want me to come get you settled in?" Mrs. Walsh offered.

"Nah!" all three said in unison.

Chloe smiled to herself. No tears in this group.

"Let's go, dudes!" Val yelled and started dribbling the ball forward, lugging her bag behind her so it flipped over onto its side every third or fourth step. Chloe gave her giant duffel a tug. It didn't budge. Ugh. Why had she brought so much stuff?

"Ever heard of wheels?" Makena said, taking the other

side of Chloe's bag with a grunt. "Man, what's in here? Andrew come along as a stowaway or something?"

Chloe grinned. She had a lot of friends. Like a lot, a lot. She'd always been popular. Kids—and even adults—were envious of her parents' money and the fact that she lived in the biggest, most expensive house in town.

A lot of kids just wanted to be friends with her because of all those things. Chloe knew that.

There was something different about her Soccer Sisters. Makena and Val were Chloe's friends because they shared a passion and because they had been through so much together.

Mud. Sweat. Tears.

They won, and they lost.

Together.

Always.

There are no slackers on a soccer field, their coach often said. Everyone worked. Everyone ached after a game. Give it your all or don't play. You earned the respect and the friendship of your teammates. To Chloe, that made those friendships sacred. They were real. They had nothing to do with what she possessed. They were about what she did, who she was inside, and what she and her soccer friends shared together.

Chloe could still remember the game that had made her understand the difference between her other friends and her Soccer Sisters. It was a cold, dark, windy afternoon match in the spring. The girls were literally playing in the middle of a nor'easter. Sleet skidded sideways across the field as the girls tried to get a foot on the slippery ball. Chloe's parents were appalled that the game had not been canceled. They were convinced their daughter would come home with pneumonia, hypothermia, or a bunch of other things that end in *ia*.

It did feel a little crazy at the time, Chloe had to admit. But it was clear from the first whistle that both sides had come to *play*. The game was a battle, and that day Chloe learned that Soccer Sisters are basically warriors. Not the Hunger Games–weapons kind of warriors, but girls who will play to win and never give up. The final score was Breakers 0, Fusion 1. The Breakers may have lost, but they weren't defeated, and they had left the field more bonded than ever.

When Chloe walked the halls of school the next day and her eyes met one of her Soccer Sisters' eyes, there was a nod. An understanding.

We play for keeps.

"Hey, guys! Wait up!" a voice called. Chloe saw another teammate, Jessie, shuffling up behind her.

"Hi, Jessie," Chloe said.

"Isn't this place the coolest?" Jessie said between huffs and puffs. She could barely walk—she was so bogged down by bags, balls, a fan, a backpack, a water bottle—basically a one-girl caravan of stuff.

"You need a hand?" Makena asked.

"Nah, I'm good," Jessie said. She waved her pinkie at them—it was the only part of her body not carrying something. Picking up some speed, she moved past Makena and Chloe, heading for the dorms.

The two girls looked at each other.

"Now, *that's* embarrassing," Makena said with a smirk, giving Chloe's giant bag another tug. Soccer Sisters were also pretty competitive.

Ahead, Chloe saw Jessie pass Val with just a quick nod. As she watched, Chloe saw a piece of paper slip out of Jessie's bag and land on the walkway.

"Jessie! You dropped something!" Chloe called, but Jessie didn't hear. She turned right into the east side of the building. Val watched her go and then turned left into the west side.

Makena was watching too.

"How do you think it's going to go with those two?" Chloe asked.

Makena scrunched up her face. She knew exactly what Chloe was talking about. Over the winter, Jessie and Val had had issues. Jessie had acted like an uber-bully, convincing Val she didn't belong on the team just because she lived in a different town. Val never told anyone about the bullying until it got so bad that she considered quitting. Of course, Makena and Chloe and the rest of the Breakers never would have let that happen, but still, they had kept a protective eye on Val ever since.

"I think it will be fine. They'll never be best friends, but they're past all that," Makena said confidently. After a pause and a sigh, she added, "Or at least I hope so."

Chloe and Makena and the giant duffel finally made it to the entryway, and Chloe stooped to pick up the piece of paper Jessie had dropped. She flipped it over and saw that it was Jessie's rooming assignment sheet:

GRAYS EAST/201
I. Hardie

J. Palise

S. Wilson

She folded the paper and slipped it into the waistband of her soccer shorts.

"I hope Jessie remembers where she's headed," she muttered to herself.

Val was waiting for them at the base of the stairs, chatting with a young woman holding a clipboard who was checking off names as campers arrived. Her name was Flavia, and she said she was from Brazil. Flavia had long, dark hair, strapped down by a ponytail holder, that flared out down her back like a long, flowing skirt.

"Hi, girls," she said sweetly. "I am going to be your keeper."

"Our *what*?" Val asked with a snicker. "You're our goalie? Awesome!"

Flavia laughed and tried again. She spoke with an accent and broke up her words in a cadence that made it clear it still took a little thought for her words to come out in English.

"I am a defender," she said to Val with a light laugh and a twinkle in her eye. "But, I'm sorry to say, a terrible goalie!" She looked to be in her early twenties and was lean and fit. Chloe thought her tan, muscular calves and thighs actually looked like a dancer's legs. She liked Flavia immediately. Her smile and easy laugh conveyed a calm, warm quality.

"Are you our counselor?" Chloe asked, trying to help.

"*Sim*," Flavia said. "*Ben vindas!* That means *welcome* in Portuguese. Please go up to your rooms, unpack, and put on your shoes. We will play at four o'clock."

"We're playing today?" Chloe asked. She had assumed they would start in the morning.

"Oh yes," Flavia said. "We play and tonight we do the evaluations to make the levels. OK. Hurry. See you in one half an hour."

Chloe, Val, and Makena scrambled to their room. There were three beds in total: one single and a bunk. They each got their own dresser, desk, and bookshelf. Val scampered up to the top bunk; Chloe was happy to take the single. Looking around the tight quarters, she imagined what it would be like to live and attend school in this place. Kind of like camp all year, she guessed. Probably pretty fun. But was it hard to be away from home all the time? She'd already seen long faces and tears from some of the younger girls at World Cup Soccer Camp.

Chloe paused and searched her feelings.

Excited? Check.

Happy? Check.

Hungry? Check, *check*.

Homesick? Not at all.

Chloe felt the scratch of the paper in the waistband

of her shorts. She fished the folded paper out and tossed it onto the bottom bunk.

Naturally, Makena was the first one ready. She flopped onto the bed, and the paper flew up into the air. Chloe saw her catch it and casually give it a scan.

Chloe bent down to put on her shin guards and heard Makena gasp. She sucked in her breath as if she had just eaten a giant bug, sat up, and banged her head on the top bunk.

"*Uhhh! No!*"

"What?" Chloe asked, trying to remember what the paper said.

"It can't be."

"What can't be?"

"This can't be right. It just can't. Val, is this right? *Thiscan'tberight!*" Makena yelled, taking no breaths.

Val had gone down the hallway to check out the bathrooms. Makena's eyes were bugging out of her head as she scanned the paper, looking at it again and again as if doing so might change the letters.

"What's the matter?" Chloe asked, trying to sound calm.

"I cannot believe it," Makena repeated, still ignoring Chloe's question. She got up, started toward the door, and ran right smack into Val, banging her in the leg.

"Ouch!"

"Here!" Makena shoved the paper at Val.

"What?" Val asked, rubbing her knee. "What's the matter?"

"This." Makena said. "*This* is the matter. Look."

"OK, I'm looking," Val said in a bored voice.

Chloe moved to read over her shoulder. Suddenly, Val looked up.

"Duuude," she said ominously.

"'Dude,' what?" Chloe asked. "Why are you saying 'dude' like that? That's a bad 'dude.'"

"No. Way," Val said, looking at Makena. "Are you serious?"

Makena nodded.

"Are you sure?" Val said.

Makena continued nodding, stunned and speechless.

Now Chloe was getting mad. Why were they so upset? The paper just had Jessie's rooming assignment. She looked again.

Val turned to Chloe, shook her head, and said, "This is not awesome."

Makena exploded. "Not awesome? *Not awesome? This is terrible!*"

Enough. Chloe grabbed Makena by the shoulders and looked her square in the eye.

"*Will one of you please tell me what the heck is going on here?*"

M akena seemed to have lost the ability to communicate. She just looked at Chloe, wide-eyed.

"It's Skylar," Val said in a flat tone.

"Skylar?" Chloe asked. The name seemed familiar, but she could hardly imagine why her friends were totally freaking out.

"Skylar," Makena said with a nod, like she was uttering the name of a very bad dog. She sat down on the bed and morosely held up the sheet, pointing to the name: S. Wilson.

Chloe narrowed her eyebrows, concentrating. Skylar? Skylar?

"Skylar from New Jersey Skylar," Val said, and then it hit Chloe like a ball to the belly.

"Ohhhh, *that* Skylar," Chloe said sympathetically. "That *is* not awesome. You're right."

Last year, Skylar Wilson had been a guest player for the Breakers during a summer tournament in Canada. A strong player their coach had somehow known, she was supposed to come and play in just a few games. But the girls soon found out that she lived by a different set of rules. Bad ones.

One toxic player had affected the whole team to a shocking degree. But most of all, she had affected Makena. Makena had been sucked in and, in trying to be cool like Skylar, had broken just about every rule about what it meant to be a Soccer Sister. She and Skylar snuck out of the team's hotel, played terribly (Makena missed an important penalty kick), lied to Makena's mom, and even ran away to New York City for a day. Makena nearly got herself kicked off the team. Of all the trouble Makena had been in over the years—and there was plenty—the summer of Skylar was by far the worst.

The last anyone had heard of Skylar, she had pulled the fire alarm in the Toronto hotel where all the teams were staying. All heck broke loose. As usual, Skylar tried to deny it, but the security cameras busted her once and for all. She was sent home from the tournament, never to be heard from again.

Until now.

In Grays East.

Right across the hall.

Oh boy. Chloe looked at the list again.

Grays East/201

I. Hardie

J. Palise

S. Wilson

Who was the third girl? she wondered.

Val wasn't looking too happy either. Chloe couldn't tell if it was because she was feeling sympathetic toward Makena or if Val was doing the same math in her mind.

Jessie + Skylar = bad news.

Chloe sat down next to Makena. All three girls exhaled simultaneously.

Wow. Things at camp had just gotten very complicated.

"Girls!" a voice called from the hallway.

No one moved. The door to their room was still slightly ajar. Chloe looked up when she heard a sharp knock.

"Girls! Let's go!" It was Flavia. A puzzled look crossed her face when she saw them all sitting in a line on the bottom bunk. "Everything OK?"

"Everything's fine!" Chloe said in a fake happy voice,

gently taking Makena by the elbow and guiding her to her feet. "Come on, Mac."

Flavia gave them one last look and then continued her search for stragglers.

"Whatever you do, just ignore the girl. We're here to play soccer and have fun, and she's not going to ruin it. I promise," Chloe said.

Makena shook her head as if to banish the memories from her mind.

"Come on, Mac. I've got your back on this one," Chloe said. "Trust me. Just follow my lead. Be cool and ignore her. OK?"

"OK," Makena said. "I can do that."

"Good," Chloe said. "Let's go."

Val nodded, and the three girls followed Flavia down to the field.

They were some of the last to arrive. Ahead, Chloe could see a gathering of girls, boys, and coaches waiting on the pristine emerald pitch. At first Chloe thought it must be turf—fake grass. No fields in her town looked like that. Nope. As she got closer, she saw that it was all real. The aroma of a fresh cut still lingered in the summer air, and she could even make out the faint crisscross lines left by the mower. It was perfect.

The sight of the soccer field seemed to buoy Makena and Val. All three girls broke into a run. Chloe kept her eyes peeled for Skylar. Chloe hadn't played in the tournament with Skylar and wasn't exactly sure what she looked like, but she remembered Makena saying that Skylar had some kind of funky spiky hair. That shouldn't be hard to spot.

"Allllllriiiiightt! Everyone, listen up!" The voice of a man in a bright-orange shirt boomed out of the center of the group. "My name is Lars, and I'm the camp director. We have a terrific group of kids and coaches here, and we're going to have a great time!"

Lars was an extremely tall human being, Chloe noted. He had platinum-blond hair cut short on the sides and long on top, which added a few inches and made it appear that white grass was growing out of his head.

"I am from the Netherlands, Flavia is from Brazil, Ian is from England, Carlos is from Spain, and Charlotte is from Canada." As he spoke, Lars pointed to the impressive crew of coaches standing next to him. "First we are going to take a photo, and then we will break up into teams and play a bit. We will divide the groups by playing level so that everyone gets the chance to shine!"

Lars had all the campers line up for the photo. There must have been about eighty kids. So far, no one had spotted Skylar. *Maybe the name S. Wilson was just a coincidence*, Chloe thought. *Maybe it was Skylar's lovely twin sister.*

Chloe was so distracted that she nearly forgot to "look pretty" as they took the picture. Makena was bouncing on her toes the entire time, and Chloe couldn't tell if it was because she was aching to play or because she was looking for Skylar. Chloe had planted herself between Makena and Val, trying to keep them both calm. Soon, Flavia came down the line, handing out pinnies, the light tops they wore to divide the girls into teams. She gave out one blue, one red, then another blue, and so on. That meant Makena and Val were given blues and Chloe got a red.

Oh well, Chloe thought. *What's the big deal if I'm not on Makena and Val's team for the scrimmage?*

"Hey, losers," a voice said from behind them. "What's happening?"

Next to her, Chloe felt Makena stiffen. She turned slowly, never doubting who she was going to face.

Skylar Wilson.

"I *said*, 'Hey, losers, what's happening?'" Skylar said. She stood with her hand on her hip, leg jutted out to the side, ball in hand, and attitude clearly on high.

Chloe prayed Makena wouldn't take the bait. *Just ignore her*, Chloe willed. *Be cool, Mac, be cool.*

Jessie and another girl walked up and stood behind Skylar. Chloe had never seen the other girl, who had brown hair and a smug look on her face.

Silence filled the air, and Chloe started to relax. *Good girl, Mac.* She turned Makena around and then heard Skylar start to laugh.

"What a loser," Skylar said loudly.

Makena whirled back to face her. *Oh no*, Chloe thought.

"*Loser?* Who are you calling a loser? You're the loser. Not me. Loser."

Oh boy, Chloe thought. Hook. Line. And sinker. She should have known that not taking the bait was not part of Makena's DNA.

Before the situation could get worse, Chloe decided to try to restart things.

"Hey, I'm Chloe," she said. Noticing that Skylar and the other two girls all held red pinnies, she added, "Looks like we're all on the same squad."

Skylar paused and looked Chloe over from head to toe.

"I remember. You're the rich ballerina, right?" she said with a sneer. "Great. Just the lame teammate I was hoping for. You better not give up the ball."

Whoa. Who is this person? Chloe wondered.

Jessie and their new roommate gathered behind Skylar.

So that's how it's going to be, Chloe said to herself. *OK, fine.*

She turned to Makena and Val and said firmly, "Ignore."

Val and Makena nodded. The three girls put on their pinnies and moved out onto the field.

5

*V*amos, *vermelho!*" Flavia called as she bounded onto the field, putting on her pinny. Happily for Chloe, it was red.

There were fifteen in the group, Flavia explained, so she was going to play in to even up the teams.

"Pass!" Flavia called to Chloe, and the two began warming up. Chloe was thrilled that Flavia had chosen her to pass with. Out of the corner of her eye, she could see Skylar's glare. Skylar and Jessie grabbed another ball and moved up next to them, passing with exaggerated touches, obviously hoping to impress Flavia.

Chloe smiled and brought the ball down, studying Skylar all the while. She had a side cut, with one part of her hair long and the other half of her head shaved.

Skylar was the kind of girl who needed attention like

oxygen—Chloe could tell that immediately. Ignoring her would be fun. Chloe peered over to the other side of the field and saw Makena and Val smiling and warming up with the blues. She was glad they were away from Skylar. Chloe could handle her, she was sure.

Flavia brought the girls in and asked them which positions they usually played. She put Chloe and Isa up front as strikers with Skylar and Jessie in the midfield. Then she put one girl in goal and took another redheaded girl back to defense with her.

"What we want to see today," Flavia said, "is how you see the field. How much you understand about soccer. Today is not about showing all your moves. OK?"

The girls all nodded. Once again, Chloe found herself drawn to Flavia. *She's simple but direct*, Chloe thought, feeling relieved. Fancy moves were not Chloe's specialty, though she did her best when she could set up the plays. But she made a lot more assists than goals, and she liked that role.

This was going to be great, Chloe thought, forgetting about Skylar for a second.

"Play!" Flavia called, punting the ball to the blue side of the field.

Naturally, Makena was on it, controlling the ball and scanning the field for a smart opening pass.

Chloe was used to playing against Makena and Val at practice, but this felt different. Watching the focus and intensity on Makena's face made her understand why Mac was so intimidating to opponents. Chloe moved forward, trying to force an error. She caught Makena up, but Makena was still able to get a long pass downfield. Skylar and Jessie won the ball together and connected on a few passes. Chloe had to admit that Skylar was a seriously skilled player. No wonder Makena had once been so impressed by her.

Once the girls settled down, the game fell into a rhythm. Jessie and Skylar were controlling most of the play for the red team, while Makena and Val attacked the blue goal relentlessly. The reds were extremely lucky to have Flavia on their side; it was clear she was a world-class player. Without her, they would have been losing 15–0. As it was, the reds were quickly down by two.

Chloe felt like she was barely in the game. She kept tracking back to help on defense but knew she had to stay forward in case the ball came her way. She worked to get open, but no passes arrived. Frustrated, she moved farther toward her own goal, trying to follow the action. *If I can win the ball, I'll just hold onto it until we can get numbers forward*, she thought to herself. Isa had stayed up at midfield, so she knew they were covered.

Val maneuvered skillfully through the red defense; Chloe so admired her ability to keep the ball through traffic and then make a dangerous pass. But as good as Val was, she was still no match for Flavia. Flavia intercepted, looked up, and saw that Chloe was open. She sent a beautiful chip pass that seemed to float down to Chloe's foot. Chloe turned quickly, sending the ball into space for Isa. Isa sprinted ahead, but Chloe's pass was a little too hard, and it went over the goal line. Looking back, Chloe saw Flavia nod in approval. She could feel that Flavia knew what she'd been trying to do. She'd make it perfect next time.

"Hey, ballerina," a voice called from behind her. "Why don't you get back in position and try to keep the ball on the field next time? You know, inside the white lines? Do you need a choreographer or something?" Skylar laughed at her own joke.

Chloe didn't respond. She ignored Skylar and got ready for the next play. The blue team took a goal kick, and Chloe moved wide to try to create space. This was something she was good at and a skill for which she credited her dance history. She'd been performing since she was a kid and had even been in a performance of *The Nutcracker* at Lincoln Center. She just seemed to know where she was in relation to other people. She knew how to get open.

Jessie won the ball at midfield and passed to Skylar. Chloe made a diagonal run into the box.

"To feet!" Chloe called, asking for a pass right to her. She saw Skylar look up and hesitate.

"Now!" Chloe called again. "I'm open!" But Skylar held onto the ball. She seemed to be looking around for anyone else to pass to.

"Skylar! Pass!" Chloe shouted. She was happy to ignore Skylar during a warm-up, but when she wanted the ball, she wasn't going to stay silent. Skylar dribbled a few more paces, refusing to pass to Chloe. Dumb move. Predictably, Val tracked back, swooped in, and stole the ball. Chloe saw Flavia shake her head at Skylar's selfish play.

Val ran back upfield at top speed, and Skylar gave chase. Hard. It was clear from the speed of her run she was angry and embarrassed to have been stripped of the ball. From her positioning, Chloe could see clearly that Skylar was following Val, not the ball. Skylar was a good head taller than Val, and Chloe knew that if she took her down from behind, Val could really get hurt.

Chloe willed Val to make a pass before Skylar caught her.

But Val had space, so she kept going.

Time seemed to slow down.

Chloe and Makena's eyes met.

"Pass!" Makena screamed to Val. There was no one around, but Makena just wanted Val to get rid of the ball too.

Chloe saw Skylar pull at Val's shirt. She could barely make herself watch.

"*Pass!*" Makena screamed again. Flavia saw what was about to happen too and sprinted toward Val.

Something in Makena's voice must have made Val change course. At the last possible second, just as Skylar launched herself in the air, Val pulled the ball back. Skylar's legs reached out for Val, but Val was too quick. Skylar flew through the air and landed with a thud.

Val passed the ball back to Makena, who was so relieved she let it go out of bounds. Bending, Val put her hands on her knees to catch her breath.

Flavia walked straight over to Skylar, who was picking herself up off the ground.

"Nothing from behind. Never," Flavia said firmly. "Next time, you're gone."

Skylar made a face behind Flavia's back, and Jessie giggled. Val jogged back to her own side of the field, a look on her face that showed she was unsure exactly what had happened—or almost happened.

When Flavia called for a water break, Chloe thought she might throw up.

"Make sure you keep getting open, Chloe," Flavia said as they got some water from a giant orange cooler.

"I am open," Chloe said. "They aren't passing to me."

Skylar and Jessie were a few feet away. They heard the exchange.

"I'm just not seeing her, you know?" Skylar said. "She's too far from the play."

Isa and then Jessie nodded in unison.

"I'm seeing you," Flavia responded, giving Skylar a sharp look.

After the break, both sides took the field. From the look on Val's face, Chloe knew Makena had told her about Skylar's attempted takedown. Chloe shook her head. The red team was already losing 2–0, and now Makena and Val were mad. They were toast.

• • •

Sure enough, Val scored right away, shooting Skylar a look and Chloe a wink. Skylar looked more and more frustrated by the minute. Chloe worked nonstop to get open but wasn't getting anything. Finally, she stole the ball from the blue defender and broke for the goal. She heard Jessie calling for a back pass so turned and laid the ball off to her.

Jessie gathered the pass and took the ball to the end line. She sent a pretty cross, and Chloe got ready for a header. She leaped into the air. She was wide open. There were no defenders near her.

But at the last second, another body got in front of her, knocking her to the side and clipping her above the eye with an elbow. Chloe couldn't believe it. It was Skylar, going for the same ball. She'd jumped right in front of Chloe.

Skylar connected with a header, directing the ball right past the keeper. Chloe lay on the ground, stunned, holding her eye and watching as her team gathered around to congratulate Skylar.

The whistle blew. The scrimmage was over.

Skylar shook her head as she walked past Chloe.

"Stick to dancing."

H ow's the shiner?" Val asked.

"Could be worse, I guess," Chloe said. She turned to face Makena and Val, who tried to hide their reactions.

"Oh, it's way better," Makena said, clearly lying.

"Totally," Val said with a nervous nod of her head.

Chloe peered into the mirror. The swelling had gone down, and the redness was fading. That was the good news. But Chloe could see traces of purple and yellow creeping in and down the side of her cheek.

Serious bad news.

She'd managed to dodge most of the picture taking over the past few days, but if she didn't show up on the camp's blog soon, her mother was going to freak. And if she showed up with an ugly shiner, she was going to freak even harder.

"You guys have any cover-up?" Chloe asked.

"Any what?" Makena said.

"You know, cover-up. Makeup?"

"Makeup?" Makena said. "At soccer camp?"

Val and Makena looked at each other and started laughing.

Chloe rolled her eyes. Should have known better than to ask her two tomboy friends. She looked over at her second suitcase. Her dance performance kit, with all sorts of foundations and powders, was inside. But she couldn't bring herself to open the bag.

I just have to turn my head when they try to take my picture next time, she thought.

Sighing at her reflection in the mirror, she started to braid her hair. Maybe the shiner would make her look tough? She made a face. Nope. She just looked a little battered.

Kind of the way she felt.

The last two days had been a drag. After the scrimmage, the coaches had basically decided to keep the two teams the same for morning training sessions. That meant Val and Makena and the blue team practiced on one field while Skylar, Jessie, Isa, and Chloe practiced on a different field. They were brought together for evening and afternoon sessions, but mornings were awful.

It was clear that the blue team had the most talented players, which left Skylar fuming. Every morning, she asked to be moved to the blue team. She made no effort to hide her opinion that the red team was way beneath her.

"We've got the ballerina," Chloe kept hearing her mutter.

Each time, Flavia and the Canadian coach, Charlotte, shook their heads and gave Skylar back her red pinny. Then, for two hours, Skylar flounced, pouted, and plotted revenge against Makena and Val. She was a nightmare, fouling, taking dives, and taunting Chloe relentlessly.

Chloe was still employing her ignore tactics, but without her usual supporters behind her, ignoring wasn't as effective. She was sick of Skylar.

Just focus on soccer, she kept telling herself. The morning session was usually small-sided drills, and Flavia was focusing on one-on-ones—which were exactly what they sounded like. One girl with the ball tries to get past one defender. When it was her turn, Chloe knew she had to keep the ball close, approach at speed, and make her move when the time was right. Chloe didn't have the best skills in the group, but she did have the longest legs. If she could get the ball behind the defender, she was off to the races.

She'd been able to beat most of the players. Except Skylar.

For some reason, when she was up against Skylar, Chloe would hesitate at the crucial moment every time. Just an instant of a second, but Skylar would strip her of the ball. Then the next time, Chloe would overcompensate, go too fast, and lose control.

Every time it happened, Skylar taunted her. Chloe had never had to play against anyone who trash-talked like Skylar did. The thing was, Skylar kept her voice low, so only Chloe could really hear her.

"Not gonna happen, Princess," she would say. Or "Give it up" or something stupid like that.

The only part of the morning Chloe liked was Flavia. Flavia was their trainer for the morning session, which meant Chloe was with her all day. At night, they all hung out together in the common area. Chloe, Makena, and Val would play card games with Flavia. Skylar, Jessie, and Isa watched TV or played their own games. Everyone could feel the tension in the air, and Chloe knew it was only a matter of time before it broke.

The previous night, after their session, Chloe had asked Flavia if she could give her some one-on-one coaching. Chloe was determined to beat Skylar before camp was over.

Now there was a knock on the door. Makena sprang

up to answer it. She came back with a plain white envelope and handed it to Chloe.

"What's this?" Chloe asked, opening the envelope, which was unsealed.

"Well, can't be too top secret," Val said. "They didn't even bother to close it."

Chloe pulled out a single piece of paper and sighed.

"It's an email from my brother," she said, curious.

The campers could receive emails that were printed and delivered to them.

"Are you sure it's not for Valeee?" Makena teased.

Val punched Makena in the arm, and the two girls immediately started wrestling on the bed.

"Will you two just go to dinner? Figure out what we're doing for the skit night. I'll meet you there," Chloe said, surprised at how thrilling it was to get a letter from home.

Makena and Val tumbled out into the hallway. "We'll save you a seat!" Val called back.

When they were gone, Chloe unfolded the letter and read:

Hey, Sis,

How's camp going?

So as part of my writing assignment, I'm supposed to keep you posted on all the (not) exciting stuff you are missing here at home. My teacher, Mrs. Bergman, is making me write it following the Rule of Three. Look it up if you want to know what the heck that means, but basically I'll give you three updates, and then I'm outie.

1) Pretty good job on the photos. Mom is scanning them like a hawk though, so you better start smiling unless you want an in-person. In the one from the first day of camp, she said she thought you had a fake smile. Then yesterday, she didn't like that your hair was in your face (and it looked dirty), but it worked well enough. She didn't see you in any pictures last night (which is why I have to write you an email), so she's expecting something good today. Oh yeah, and she said to put on more sunblock. Says you are getting too many freckles or something about the color of your face. I know, annoying.

2) Kittygate continues. Smitty knocked Mom's water glass over in the middle of the night, and it landed right on her head. She

screamed so loud I thought the fire alarm was going off. Dad laughed until he cried, and while I was seriously afraid for him (Mom was not amused), it was good to hear him cracking up like that. Cat is growing on me.

3) Karl and I went to the pier but didn't have any luck. I did bring home some of the stinky bait, and Mom busted Dad trying to hand-feed his kitten. Priceless!

4) The coach from the Rough Riders asked me to play at a tourney next weekend. This is the club I was telling you about. I hope the guys are cool. I know they are really awesome players. The jamboree is in a town pretty close to your camp, Mom said. (Alert, alert!)

Well, I guess that was four things instead of three. Guess that's why I still need a math tutor. Catch ya later.

Your super awesome
big bro,
A

PS Say hi to Val for me.

Smiling, Chloe reread her brother's email a few times. Then she carried it with her to the common room computer to respond. The place was totally deserted; it was taco night in the cafeteria.

She thought for a minute before she began to type.

Dear Bro,

Thanks for the email. Everything is going GREAT. The coaches are super cool, and I've made a ton of friends. Friday night is the big skit night, and Makena, Val, and I are going to do something cool. Tell Mom not to worry and that I AM putting on sunblock! If you take the cat hostage, I bet you could get Dad to take you fishing. Or, actually, Mom. LOL!

Love,
C

Chloe looked at her email and sighed. Not exactly the whole truth. But still. Even if she had a black eye and felt miserable most of the time, there was no way she was ever going to admit that to her parents or anyone else.

7

Chloe snuck out of Room 204 West while Makena and Val were still snoozing. She grabbed an apple from the common room table and bopped down the stairs and out the door, breathing in the warm, moist summer air. The dew-covered grass shimmered in the early-morning light. The sun was over the horizon already.

Flavia was sitting on a bench, her face raised to the sky like a lizard on a rock.

"Morning," Chloe said.

"*Bom dia!*" Flavia said with a smile, closing her eyes again and lifting her face to the sun. She didn't seem too anxious to get moving, so Chloe sat down next to her on the wooden bench and took a bite of her apple. She could hear Flavia's relaxed breathing. Soon enough, she closed her own eyes. She loved the warmth on her face and the stillness all around them.

A bird whistled nearby, and Flavia finally spoke. "This is my favorite part of the day, when the birds are the only ones talking."

Chloe laughed and made sure to chew quietly. She'd never thought about mornings in that way before. She'd never really thought about them much at all. Most of her early hours were filled with sleep or chaos, rushing to get to school or practice. She didn't think she'd ever woken up and just listened to the day begin.

"When I was a little girl," Flavia continued, "early morning was the only time it was quiet. Just the roosters had something to say."

"You grew up on a farm?" Chloe asked, imagining a rooster's cock-a-doodle-doo, like in "Old McDonald" or something.

Flavia chuckled. "No, I didn't grow up on a farm. I grew up in a *favela*."

"A what?" Chloe asked.

"*Uma favela*," Flavia said. "It's where a lot of people live in Brazil."

"Oh," Chloe answered, unsure of what else to add. After a minute she asked, "It was loud there?"

"Not so much loud as crowded," Flavia said with a shake of her head. "There were so many people in just two rooms. I never had enough space to think! Good and bad noises."

Chloe tried to imagine what living in such close quarters would be like.

"Hard to do your homework, huh?" Chloe asked.

Flavia nodded, chuckling. "Yes, it was."

A comfortable silence filled the air. Flavia began to braid her curly black hair. When she was done, the braid reached nearly to her waist.

"I love your hair," Chloe said. "It's so long."

"Thanks," Flavia said. "I used to wear it short, like a boy's."

"You did?" Chloe asked. "Why?"

Flavia grabbed a ball and stood up. She started to juggle. "So I could play."

"You had to have short hair to play soccer?" Chloe asked, confused.

Flavia grinned at Chloe and kept on juggling but didn't respond. It was like the ball was on a string attached to her foot, her thigh, even her head. Chloe had already lost count of how many taps Flavia had done. *Wow*, she thought.

"Is that why your hair is so long now?" Chloe asked, watching in awe.

Flavia paused and let the ball drop. She studied Chloe

for a minute. "You know, maybe that is why I don't like to cut it. I never realized this." Flavia grabbed her braid and twisted it around her finger. "I will explain. I had to keep my hair short so I could play with the boys. I hoped none of the mothers noticed that I was a girl playing soccer. Now come on," she said, changing the subject.

Chloe stood. Flavia gently tapped the ball over to her. Chloe juggled easily, letting the ball land on each foot and then her thighs, finally using her head a few times. She'd been practicing all summer and was even learning some freestyle juggling moves. After a while, she tapped the ball gently back to Flavia.

Flavia nodded her approval. "Not bad, not bad at all." She peered at Chloe's face. "How's the eye?"

"Purple," Chloe said.

Flavia nodded and laughed. "Yes, it is."

They juggled for a while longer and then started passing. Flavia's touches were light and fast.

"So where do you live?" Flavia asked. "How many brothers and sisters do you have?"

"I live two hours from here. Close to New York City. And I have one brother named Andrew. He's older than I am. So it's just me, my mother, my brother, my father…oh, and our new kitten," Chloe said.

Wow, we have a pet, she realized. *That's new. My family sounds almost normal.*

"How about you?" Chloe added. "Do you have any brothers and sisters?"

Flavia nodded and held up her hand. "Five brothers."

"Wow."

"All older. They are the ones who taught me to play and who let me play. Girls in Brazil aren't supposed to play *futebol*. I wanted to look just like one of my brothers so the other mothers wouldn't say bad things about me."

"My parents don't really want me to play soccer," Chloe said, feeling suddenly like she could tell Flavia anything.

"Why not?" Flavia asked, confused. "I thought American parents love to make their children play sports to pay for college."

"Well, they think I should just do ballet. My mom says it's more appropriate for girls," Chloe said and made a sour face.

"Ah, a ballerina. That is why Skylar says those things to you," Flavia said.

"Yes, I dance. But I don't know why Skylar cares so much."

"Jealous," Flavia said flatly. "Are you a good dancer?"

Chloe shrugged her shoulders but then nodded. "Yeah, I am."

Flavia stopped passing. "And an excellent juggler. You are…smooth," she said, looking like she was searching for a better word in English. "*Graciosa*, we say in Brazil. Like the large bird. The goose?"

Chloe laughed. "I hope I am more *graciosa* than a goose!"

"No. Not the goose. *Un cisne*. The white bird with the spot and the black face."

"Oh, a swan! That's much better," Chloe said.

"I believe you are a great dancer," Flavia said.

Flavia backed up and started sending long chips in the air, hitting the ball with just the perfect amount of back-spin so that it almost stopped right at Chloe's feet. Then Flavia showed Chloe how to lock her foot in place and hit the bottom of the ball so that it floated gently in the air. They were too far apart to continue their chat, but as they passed back and forth, Chloe thought about all they had said to one another.

Being called graceful should have made her happy, but honestly, she was more excited that Flavia thought she was a good juggler. Chloe wondered why she found so much more joy in soccer than in ballet. By comparison, there was no comparison. She was a much better dancer. Her mother was right about that at least. She really could be a prima ballerina if she wanted to be.

The ball came back at her, this time much higher. Chloe had to back up and adjust her positioning in order to receive the pass. Everything in ballet was preplanned. Choreographed. Where she stood, how she held her fingers, where she focused her eyes; every single step predetermined. Judged.

Chloe hated the constant comparisons, whether good or bad, to other dancers. She couldn't stand being unable to create her own plan; she hated always trying to be as good as or better at doing what others had done before her.

Soccer was a different kind of dance. Every move or decision was a reaction to the play, the ball, or a teammate. In every game, drill, or practice, the weather could change; the field could be wet or the gym floor slippery and hard. The players had to adjust accordingly. Chloe loved the freedom of soccer, the freedom to be creative with your body and your mind, the challenge of syncing that creativity with your teammates.

To her, when it all worked, there was no dance more beautiful in the world. Chloe's frustrations began to ease. She felt light and happy. And she felt grateful to Flavia. Despite coming from a totally different world, the counselor was helping Chloe understand her own.

"Can we do this again tomorrow, Flavia?"

"*Claro que sim*," Flavia said. "We will do this every day if you want, Goose."

8

Chloe felt lighter. She'd always been pretty graceful, or *graciosa*, as Flavia said, but after their talk, she felt like she was flying across the field. Creative. Free. Light on her toes. She unleashed some of her most daring moves, the ones she usually only tried alone in her backyard, including "The Maradona," named after a famous Argentine player. She didn't get to go one-on-one with Skylar, but she did smoke Jessie, which was satisfying enough.

She'd felt such an instant, strong bond to Flavia, like a magnet on a refrigerator. There was a comfort between them despite their differences in age and background. The same shared love of the game, Chloe guessed. And shared frustration when people or things got in the way of that love.

Chloe practically skipped into the crowded cafeteria, scanning the faces for Makena and Val. The commissary was buzzing with excitement. It was as if someone had sprinkled sugar next to an anthill. The girls were scampering up to one another, exchanging information, and passing it along to the next girl. Soccer gossip pheromones. Chloe laughed as she picked up snippets of the conversations flowing from the salad bar to the dessert table.

"We're playing another camp? Which one?" chirped an impish girl named Bella.

"Will college coaches be there?" asked a beautiful camper named Katie Moore. Katie wore crimson shorts and socks every day because she was obsessed with playing at Harvard. She had already announced to the entire camp that she was going to study English and marry a hockey player.

"They're going to videotape it!" exclaimed Lauren, one of the older girls and, in Chloe's opinion, one of the better players.

Three major developments were brewing, it seemed. First, a girl named Kiana had broken her wrist playing soccer tennis, a game in which a soccer ball was used on a tennis court. Kiana went for a ball and ran into the net, landing on her wrist. She ended up with a hairline fracture. Oh, and she was a goalie—so hands mattered.

The second topic of chatter was skit night. All the campers were invited to get up onstage and perform a funny scene. Chloe was used to performing, so this wasn't that scary for her, but most of the camp was freaking out. She, Makena, and Val were going to plan their skit at lunch. They had two days to figure something out.

Only the third development really grabbed Chloe's attention: Lars, the camp director, had announced at the start of the morning session that the neighboring Soccer Stars camp had challenged World Cup Camp to a tournament day. The games would be played in front of parents and incoming campers during the halfway point of camp on visitors' day. There might even be some college scouts for the older girls.

Chloe kept moving. She wasn't surprised to find Makena and Val bickering by the drink station.

"Val, you can't put ice in milk," Chloe heard Makena say authoritatively.

"Why not?" Val asked. "Who made that rule?"

"It's just weird," Makena said. She spotted Chloe. "It's weird, right, Chloe? And gross. I mean, who puts ice in their milk?"

Chloe shrugged. "Never tried it."

Makena shook her head in disgust. "I don't get this new milk thing, Val. I really don't."

Val just smiled and added more crushed ice to her cup,

making a face behind Makena's back. Chloe giggled at her friend's recent obsession. The cafeteria had a milk dispenser that allowed you to pick from skim, one percent, two percent, vanilla, and chocolate. As if that wasn't fun enough, Charlotte the Canadian had told Val during a nutrition session that milk was good for strong bones. Ever since, Val had been obsessed with milk—and now apparently ice too.

"I'm going to grow an inch at least!" Val said. "Next I think I'm going to put some orange juice in my milk."

"Seriously?" Chloe asked. That was a new one.

"Oh, sure. It's a Mexican drink. My dad taught me about it."

"You're going to get a stomachache," Makena said. "And worse gas than you already have."

Chloe shook her head and laughed. She had to agree with Makena on that one. Being roommates with her Soccer Sisters was a whole new level of closeness, some of it the smelly kind. But Val was undeterred. Chloe watched as she filled her glass with ice and milk and then topped it off with orange juice.

When Val was midway through drinking the beverage, the crushed ice became a giant ball and detached from the bottom of the glass. It crashed into Val's face, coating her nose and eyebrows with cold orange milk.

Makena guffawed and doubled over laughing. "Nice one!"

"Dude!" Val cried, looking around for something to use to wipe her face.

Chloe grabbed a few napkins and handed them over.

"Maybe that should be your act for skit night, Val. How to take a milk shower?"

"I think it's in my nose," Val said in a funny voice. Liquid continued to drip off her face.

Since Makena and Val already had their food, Chloe moved to the sandwich bar. She had to admit that the food at World Cup Camp was delicious.

She sat down again with Makena and Val, who were debating the merits of chocolate versus vanilla milk.

"Vanilla milk is lame," Makena said. "It's either plain or chocolate in my book."

"Makena, I never knew you were such a milk expert," Chloe said with a laugh.

"Yeah, well, I never knew anyone who talked about milk as much as this one over here. She's part cow now."

Time to change the subject. "So what do you think about the Soccer Stars game?"

"I heard the director of that camp used to work here and hates Lars. Her name is Chumeta, and Lars apparently hates her right back. But…" Val brought her face down low to the table, contributing her own dose of gossip in a deep, serious tone. "Some of the other girls were saying that they're secretly in loooooove."

"Well, I think it sounds awesome," Chloe said. "I know we'll kill them."

"We?" An unwelcome voice had joined the conversation. "We're not dancing the Nutbreaker."

"Nut what?" Chloe said with a scowl. Of course, it was Skylar who stood behind them, a tray held above her head. She pulled out a chair and scowled at Chloe.

"You're not even going to make it on the field. You know that Lars wants to win, so he's *def* only going to field the best players."

Skylar and Jessie put their food down, as if to join the girls at the table. Chloe was so stunned by what Skylar had just said that she slumped back in her chair without trying to stop them.

"Hey, Skylar," Makena said. "Why don't you butt out?"

"Just being honest," Skylar said with a fake smile.

But Makena wasn't done. Chloe knew the animosity between the two was still hot. Trouble was brewing.

"Go sit somewhere else," Makena said firmly. "No one wants you here."

Skylar was momentarily silenced by Makena's attack. Jessie looked ready to come to Skylar's defense, but before she could speak, Chloe recovered enough to shoot her a prime Chloe glare. Hopefully Jessie was smart enough to remember that after this camp was over, she was going back to the Breakers and Brookville.

It worked. Jessie stayed quiet and slid her tray farther down the table, gesturing for Skylar to follow.

Quiet tension remained in the air until Skylar followed.

"So what skit do you guys want to do?" Val asked. Chloe could tell she was trying to change the subject. Chloe sank lower in her chair. She picked up her turkey sandwich but had no appetite. She put it back down again.

"I think we should do the talk show thing," Makena said. "You know, where we pretend to be the coaches being interviewed on a talk show?" She stuck a white napkin on her head, sat up stiffly in her chair, and said in a deep voice, "Well, allllllllllllrighty then…"

"That's an awesome Lars imitation!" Val cheered. "We must, must, must do, do, do!"

Chloe smiled but could only shrug her shoulders. She whispered to Makena and Val, "Do you think Skylar is right? That I won't get to play in the game?"

What would her mother say if she came to a game and Chloe didn't even get to play? She didn't want to imagine it. Makena cast her eyes down. Chloe looked at Val. She wasn't sure she wanted to hear the truth.

Val shrugged and whispered, "I bet everyone will play. Don't worry about it."

Chloe saw Jessie and Skylar leaning toward them, trying to listen in on their conversation. The last thing she wanted was for Skylar to know she worried she might not be good enough to get into the game.

"So about skit night!" Chloe said, loudly changing the subject.

"Oh, I can do a mean Flavia impression!" Jessie said suddenly, speaking from down the table. Chloe was surprised that Jessie was attempting to be civil but happy to see her at least trying.

"*Git tua de pelota!*" she said in a squeaky voice.

Skylar laughed loud and hard. "OMG, I can barely understand anything she says! She's always speaking Spanish," she said.

Unfortunately for Val, she had just gulped a giant mouthful of Mexican orange milk. Chloe saw her eyes bulge. Val tried to swallow, but her mouth was too full, so Chloe stepped in for her.

"Uh, first of all, I can understand her perfectly. And second of all, she speaks Portuguese, not Spanish, Skylar."

"Whatever! Spanish. Portuguese. It's all the same to me. Hey, Jessie, I have an idea for—"

Suddenly a giant spray of milk covered the table. Val's eruption.

"Duuuuuuuude! You are a total idiot!" Val stood up and shouted at Skylar, unconcerned by the fact that she had just drenched the entire table.

"Oh. No. You. Didn't," Skylar said, a glare in her eye and milk in her hair. She was soaked. She stood and lifted her hand to her face. "I'm going to get you. All of you!"

OMG. Chloe thought to herself. *This can't happen.*

Val reached for her glass. Which was huge and still pretty full.

Makena moved to intervene.

"Everyone, knock it off!" She grabbed for Val's arm, but Val dodged and Makena's hand landed on the table. Her fingers inadvertently smacked her fork, which shot up and sprayed a pile of taco meat onto Jessie's lap.

Makena froze.

"Uh…"

It was too late. Jessie and Skylar looked at one another,

and without another word, Skylar threw her glass of lemonade right into Makena's face.

Chloe sucked in her breath.

"No! No! No!" she yelled.

It was no use. Val let the rest of her iced Mexican orange milk fly. Skylar and Jessie ducked, and it flew forward through the air. Chloe watched the milk mess move like an orange octopus in slow motion, hitting at least eight different girls in the cafeteria. Lauren took some right in the eye. Her tray clattered to the ground, salad covering the floor like seaweed.

Bella yelled, "*Food fight!*"

Chicken cutlets started flying. Pizza missiles landed on the wall.

Chloe stood, mouth agape. Makena and Val tried to back out of the room, ducking as orange slices whizzed by, and Chloe moved to join them.

Wisely, Skylar and Jessie ran.

Edible pandemonium reigned. It was like a scene from an old movie Chloe's father would have liked.

"Dude!" Val screeched as an apple nearly took off her head.

"Let's get out of here," Makena said. They kept inching toward the door, backing up so as to keep their eyes open.

They didn't notice that the entire coaching staff had just come running into the room.

Lars stepped forward, his face red with fury. Chloe heard him mutter something in Dutch, take a deep breath, and scream: "*Cut! It! Out!*"

Chloe's eyes met Flavia's.

Her mentor was shaking her head in disgust.

I t was bad. No matter how many times Chloe tried to explain that all the chaos had started by mistake, Lars kept shaking his head and rubbing his platinum-blond hair. He seemed to be doing the "relaxation breathing" she had seen her mother try once. Long inhales through the nose, longer exhales through the mouth.

In.

Out.

The outs sounded like someone had cracked open a car window while speeding along a highway.

Val, Makena, and Chloe kept looking at one another. The only sound in the room was Lars's wheezy breaths. There was nothing more to say.

After the next inhale, Lars finally exhaled a sad and

quiet "Alrighty then." He rose slowly and turned to talk with Flavia and Charlotte.

"Everyone will meet back in the cafeteria," he said after a minute, this time in a slightly louder tone.

Chloe wasn't sure what to do. She looked at Makena and Val, who both shrugged their shoulders. No one moved a muscle.

"Now!" Lars bellowed.

All three girls took off at a sprint. Naturally, Val was first, with Makena and Chloe right behind. They pulled up when they got to the cafeteria, which looked like it had been coated from floor to ceiling in rainbow paint.

"Dude," Val muttered in a low voice. The three girls slunk in and joined the rest of the campers, who were huddled in a corner. Chloe thought they looked like a kennel of guilty dogs. Eyes on the ground. Heads down. She felt the same way. *If we had tails, they'd be between our legs*, Chloe thought.

"What'd he say?" one of the younger girls asked.

"Nothing," Chloe whispered back.

"Scary," the little girl said.

Chloe nodded.

"What's he going to do to us?" Bella asked.

"I have no idea," Chloe responded truthfully.

"It's all your fault," the little girl said, and Chloe recoiled. "I only chucked my lime Jell-O at Kiana."

Was that what everyone in the camp believed? That the massive food fight was her fault? Chloe suddenly felt sick to her stomach—and the feeling had nothing to do with the sticky glob of ketchup coating her shoe.

All the coaches silently filed in. The only sound was the rolling of soccer cleats on linoleum.

Chloe studied Lars's face. He was still a reddish hue, but he seemed to be breathing normally. The other coaches looked like they were trying not to laugh. All of them except Flavia. Her eyes were red, and Chloe saw her wipe her face on her sleeve. *Why is she so upset?* Chloe wondered.

"Campers," Lars said. "This is a very disappointing day at World Cup Camp. Look around you."

The girls did. *It really is an impressive scene of destruction*, Chloe thought with a wince.

"Never before have we had a situation like this," Lars said. "It will take us some time to decide what the punishment should be. But I have heard the explanations for how it began."

Chloe felt a poke in her side from the younger girl. *Gee, how about some respect for your elders?* she thought, shooting the kid a glare.

Lars looked at the campers. "I am unmoved," he said.

Chloe felt tears well up in her eyes. Unmoved? What the heck did that mean?

Punishment?

What were they going to do to them? To whom exactly was he talking?

"First thing, we are going to clean this mess up. And when I say *we*, I mean *you*, all of you. Whether you were involved or not. We will use this as a lesson about being on a team."

Lars bent down to pick up a piece of soggy bread from the floor in front of him. He walked to a garbage can and paused before dropping it in.

"Whether you threw this lettuce," he said, pointing to the wall, "or that spaghetti. Or nothing. There is no way to know. So every one of you will have the same punishment, and every one of you will clean. Afternoon sessions will be canceled to allow you time to compose emails to your parents. You will explain what has happened. Each camper will print a copy of her sent email and leave it on my desk. Then we will do some running.

"We will meet tonight to discuss what further steps need to be taken. You may not have realized that this is a private school. The school generously allows us to use its facilities during the summer. Incidents like this put the whole camp in jeopardy. While I understand that soccer players are generally high-spirited, this abusive behavior will not be tolerated. Anyone caught not cleaning up will be immediately sent home. Anyone caught breaking any other rules will be immediately sent home."

He dropped the bread into the garbage can with a hollow thump. Chloe scanned the crowd, searching the sea of faces.

"Where's Skylar?" she whispered to Makena. "And Jessie?"

Makena shrugged.

Lars continued his lecture. "Soccer is a game of respect. Respect for the rules, respect for the players, respect for the coaches, and, yes, even for the referees."

The girls gave a tentative chuckle. Lars didn't smile, but some of the other coaches did.

"Mops and buckets are in the custodian's closet. You have one hour to clean up every single scrap of food. We will meet again for evening session at five o'clock."

With that, Lars turned and walked out the door.

O K. Here goes," Chloe said, pressing the Send button on the computer. Then she pressed Print and listened for the purr of the machine.

Makena and Val were waiting by the door, worried looks on their faces. They held their printed emails to their parents in their hands.

"Have you guys seen Skylar or Jessie yet?" Makena asked.

Val shook her head.

"I haven't seen them print or write any emails yet. And they didn't help clean up either." Makena sounded concerned.

Chloe grabbed her email from the printer and then turned. "Who cares where they are?"

"We should turn them in for not helping," Val said cheerfully.

Chloe liked the sound of that. Though she was fed up with Skylar, it was Jessie who had really set her off. Jessie was supposed to be one of her Soccer Sisters. The speed with which she'd dropped her teammates to hang out with Skylar amazed Chloe. She wouldn't forget Jessie's betrayal anytime soon. At school, Jessie was constantly circling Chloe, trying to get into her group of friends.

We'll see about that, Chloe thought.

"Let's go," Chloe said, catching up to Makena and Val. They were all wearing their camp shirts and shorts, but Flavia had stopped by to tell them not to bother putting on their cleats for practice. Chloe didn't like the sound of that.

"So why aren't we wearing cleats?" she said out loud. "I mean, we already cleaned up the mess. What else?"

Makena shrugged her shoulders, but Val raised her eyebrows knowingly.

"I'm sure we're about to find out," she said.

Chloe sighed in resignation, and they crossed the beautiful campus green toward Lars's office. As ordered, they would drop off printed copies of their emails home before heading out to the fields.

"Man, it's hot today," Chloe said, feeling a trickle of sweat run down her back. She noticed other groups of campers ahead of them on their way to the same office, a cramped room on the far side of the main campus library. Each one carried a single white piece of paper.

"Do you think everyone knows we started the food fight?" Makena asked.

"Technically, we did not start it," Val said. "I was just reacting to Skylar being the biggest idiot on the planet."

Makena gave Val a look.

Chloe frowned. "You did kind of toss your magic milk across the room, Val."

"She trounced me with lemonade!"

"I know, I know, but…" Chloe let the sentence fade.

"Let's face it," Makena said. "We're definitely not the most popular kids at camp right now."

Chloe looked down at her email.

Dear Mom and Dad,

There was a small incident in the school cafeteria today. I participated in a food fight and am very sorry for my actions. I did help clean up the mess and have been advised that "any other violations of camp regulations will result in my being sent home."

Having a great time! No need to come
and visit!

Love,
Chloe

"My parents are not going to like this at all," Chloe said quietly.

"Oh well. My parents are just going to shrug and say, 'Here we go again,'" Makena said with a laugh.

"My dad will be shocked," Val admitted. "But, you know, I think he might actually be relieved!"

Makena laughed again and threw her arm around Val's shoulder. "It is kind of refreshing not to be the *only* one in trouble all the time!"

"I can hear my dad now," Chloe said with a sigh. "*A Gordon involved in outrageous behavior?*" She stood up tall and tucked in her chin. "*That is unacceptable, young lady.*"

Still arm in arm, Makena and Val broke into fits of laughter. Chloe shook her head and sighed. "I can only hope that Andrew intercepts the message for me."

"Whose email did you send it to?" Val asked, peering over Chloe's shoulder to read.

"His!" Chloe laughed.

Val giggled. "I'm sure he'll cover for you on this one."

"Yeah, but you're going to owe him big-time!" Makena said as they approached the office door.

"I'll promise him a date with Val," Chloe said with a smirk, earning herself an immediate shove from behind. But she could see Val smiling as they left the office.

All grinning halted when they got to the field.

First of all, there was only one coach: Lars. Second of all, there were no balls and no cones, which meant there were no games to be played.

"On the line, girls!" Lars said as soon as the campers had gathered.

Out of the corner of her eye, Chloe saw Jessie and Skylar glaring at her from the other side of the group.

All the girls took a spot on the end line.

"Well, alrighty then. We're going to focus on fitness this afternoon," Lars said. His words were immediately followed by a collective groan from the girls.

"We will start with suicides."

Louder groans.

"With *what*?" one of the younger campers shouted in alarm. "It was just a food fight!"

Lars tried not to smile, but Chloe saw the sides of his mouth twitching slightly.

"Suicide sprints. This is what they are called in English. But perhaps you are right, and we should not use this term. Another name for this activity is *gassers*, so we will use this word instead."

A murmur of dismayed chuckles rippled through the group. Chloe knew what gassers were. Like all soccer players on planet Earth, she hated them. Coach Lily sometimes made the Breakers do the exercises: she put four cones in a line, about five yards apart; the team then had to sprint to the first one, sprint back to the line, sprint to the second one, then sprint back to the line, continuing this pattern with all four cones.

Fitness might be a vital part of the game, but most soccer players felt the way Chloe did: *If we wanted to do sprints, we'd join the track team instead.* Gassers were just brutal. To make it worse, the sun was beating down so fiercely that Chloe thought she could feel it burning her skin through her thin camp T-shirt.

Lars was carrying a brown bag under one arm. He must have the cones in there, she thought.

"Please begin with jumping jacks," Lars said. "I will teach you today to count in Dutch. We do not have to warm up very much, as it is already very warm outside."

A snicker passed through the group.

"Let us begin. One, *een*, two, *twee*, three, *drie*…"

The girls were giggling by the time they finished, and Chloe was starting to feel less worried. Maybe this won't be so bad after all, she thought. She wiped sweat from her brow and squinted into the glaring late-afternoon sun, wishing for rain.

"Now that we are warmed up, we will start with the sui…uh, with the gassers."

"But where are the cones?" one of the girls asked.

"Ah, good question!" Lars said. "Instead of cones, today we will use reminders of why we are not playing soccer right now, eh?"

Chloe looked on in horror as Lars pointed to a pile of garbage bags.

"Is that…" Val whispered.

"Food from the food fight. Yep," Makena muttered.

"Ewww," the girls howled in protest.

"I see this has gotten your attention," Lars said with a smirk. "You will sprint to the piles of garbage today. I hope this will inspire you not to repeat today's mistake. Now, on my whistle!"

Chloe lost track of how many sprints they ran. After the suicides, they had to do 120s, sprinting the length of the soccer field, jogging back, and sprinting again, with no breaks in between the runs. The younger girls were excused after about fifteen minutes, but the older girls like Chloe, Makena, and Val were afforded no breaks.

At one point, Skylar told Lars she was going to throw up. His only response was to shrug his shoulders and point to the closest garbage can.

"Don't miss," he mumbled.

When they were finally done, the girls staggered back to their dorms, exhausted and drenched in sweat.

"I hope everyone is too tired to hate us," Makena said as they collapsed in their bunks.

"Unlikely," Val moaned.

Impossible, Chloe knew.

Chloe's legs felt like wooden boards. Stiff, rough, and unbendable. She was so sore that when she tried to stand, she had to give up and flop back down on the bed. There was literally no part of her body that didn't feel achy and exhausted.

Just half an hour more, she told herself, curling up painfully and going back to sleep.

A rhythmic ping woke her just in time for morning session, a *ting, ting, ting* that vibrated the windowpane. With a stir of relief, Chloe realized it was rain. She rubbed her legs again and heard Val and Makena start to stir.

"*Dude.*" That was enough to know that Val's legs felt as heavy as Chloe's.

"I'm scared to move," Makena said in a low voice. "My legs feel like someone is sitting on them."

"At least it's raining. Lars can't torture us anymore," Chloe said, pointing toward the window.

"That's what you think," Val said. "Rain just means we play in the gym."

"Hey, weren't you supposed to meet Flavia this morning?" Makena asked.

"Oh, right. I guess I fell back asleep," Chloe said. "But, I mean, it's raining. She probably didn't bother coming, right?"

Chloe swung her legs around and stood up. Not even a month of ballet training could test her muscles like those horrid sprints. She wondered how the rest of the camp was faring and then winced at the thought of them cursing her name as they tried to get out of bed. If they were as dog-tired as she was, maybe they wouldn't have the energy to hate her.

The three girls limped to breakfast, impressed again by how spotless the cafeteria was. They grabbed some fruit (and milk for Val) and then scurried to the gym to avoid getting soaked. The summer rain was pouring down in sheets.

There was no shortage of cones this morning, Chloe saw. Plastic circles of orange, neon-yellow, pink, red, and blue dotted the gym floor like confetti.

The rest of the campers straggled in.

"Alrighty then," Lars said, kicking off the session. "Today is a new day. A wet new day, but that's just a good chance to wash away the disappointments of yesterday and move on to the opportunities of the future!"

Chloe yawned in spite of herself.

"Today we will work on our ball skills," Lars continued. "Without them, soccer is just a game of kickball with goals. Please see Flavia for your group assignment for this session."

Chloe, Makena, and Val walked over to Flavia, who was immediately surrounded. Campers jockeyed to get close to her and find out their groups. Chloe couldn't imagine what all the fuss was about. It was just a morning session. Who cared?

She hung back, waiting for all the pushing to stop.

"I can't believe Lars is picking the team today. I hate playing in the gym," she overheard a girl near her say. "The floor is too hard. And the lighting is just so harsh. It's really not fair."

So that's why everyone was so tense, she realized. Lars was making the roster for the inter-camp game. Would she make it? Of course she wanted to, but she had to admit to herself that she probably wouldn't. Chloe looked up to inspect the lighting. It had never dawned on her to look up in a gym before. Rows of bright lights dotted the ceiling. But with the exception of a few dead bulbs, the lights seem to be doing their jobs. What was the girl complaining about? Chloe shrugged to herself, inching closer to Flavia.

"Chloe, you are with Makena and Val in the green group," Flavia said when she saw Chloe. She handed the girls green pinnies. "You'll be with me. Get warmed up by juggling over there. I'll be over as soon as I have finished with these crazy girls."

Chloe was thrilled to be with Makena and Val for a change. She turned and smiled at her friends. Maybe she did have a chance now after all!

"Let's go!" Makena said. Chloe's legs protested for the entire jog across the gym but started to loosen up once she was juggling.

"Thigh, thigh, foot, foot, head, foot, foot, thigh," Chloe whispered to herself, dropping the ball at her feet.

Using the top of her right foot, she gently guided the ball up her laces and popped it up into the air. Immediately she tapped the ball with her right thigh, then her left, let it drop down to her left foot, then to her right. She popped it up into the air and tapped it once with her head. The touch was a little too hard, and the ball went flying.

"Drat!" she said to herself, chasing the ball down.

"Hey, that was really good," Makena said. "Do you map out your juggling now?"

"Oh, sometimes," Chloe said. "I try to make a pattern to follow so it's not so random. Helps me get focused, I guess."

"What's your record these days?" Val asked.

"I don't know," Chloe thought for a second. "Like four hundred?"

"Four what?" Makena shouted. "You can juggle the ball four hundred times in a row?"

Chloe laughed. "Well, not all the time. But I can almost always get to one hundred now."

Val and Makena were staring at her, mouths open, eyes bugged.

"You know I've been working on it in my basement, right?" Chloe said. What she didn't add was that she was even thinking about competing in a freestyle juggling competition later in the summer. Freestyle was when you juggled the ball with moves as long and creatively as possible.

"I knew you were working on it, but *duuuude*, that's insane!" Val said. "My best is eighty."

"Hey, girls, how about a few juggles for the camera?" Coach Carlos asked. He was obviously photographer for the day.

Oh man, Chloe thought. With all the food fight drama, she hadn't been in a picture for more than two days. Her mom was going to freak. At least her bruise was gone. Praying that Andrew had intercepted the email she'd sent yesterday, Chloe started to juggle, feet only, delicately controlling the ball and creating a nice, easy rhythm.

Tap. Tap. Tap. Tap.

She was so focused on her juggling that she didn't even see the trainer take the picture.

Tap. Tap. Tap. Tap.

"Very impressive," Flavia said, appreciation in her voice. Chloe smiled and caught the ball. She looked around to see if Lars had been watching but couldn't see him.

"Thanks," she said. "I actually find it sort of relaxing."

"I missed you this morning," Flavia said. Chloe thought she heard a flash of coldness in her voice.

"Oh, uh…" Chloe stammered. "I…uh…I went back to bed. I'm sorry. I was so tired from the sprints."

"I was tired too," Flavia said. "But I told you I would be there, right?"

"It was raining…"

Flavia just looked at her and nodded slowly. Chloe's eyes dropped to the ground. She had let Flavia down. And been inconsiderate too.

"I'll be there next time, Flavia. I promise," Chloe said. "And I'm really sorry. Tomorrow?"

Flavia said OK and walked away. It was more than just disappointment that Chloe had missed their morning meeting. It was something else, something troubling.

After some more juggling, they practiced cone drills, starting with right-footed dribbling through the cones, which were set up in patterns meant to replicate game situations. Left-footed drills were next. Chloe struggled with her weaker foot, but after a few tries, she got more comfortable.

While foot skills were fun, the gym was like a sweatbox. A few feeble electric fans tried to stir the air, but the combination of heat, humidity, and humans had turned the gym into a sauna. Chloe was relieved when Flavia called a water break.

The girls gathered at the orange cooler, filling cup after cup with water.

"Ugh, this water tastes terrible," one of the older girls said, making spitting sounds.

"It's not even cold," echoed another. "And these cups are so small."

Chloe caught Flavia frowning as she watched the girls at the cooler from her spot on the field.

"Those are great," a girl said to Chloe as they headed

back to the center of the gym. She was admiring Chloe's neon-yellow indoor shoes. Each girl had to bring at least one pair of cleats and a pair of indoor shoes to camp. Cleats were not allowed in the gyms; they had no traction and made players slip in addition to marking up the floor.

"Thanks," Chloe said. "My mom got them for me for camp…"

Her voice trailed off. She'd forgotten that her mother had surprised her with new shoes. They were the perfect size and a really cool style. *Mom might not know much about soccer, but she can sure pick out awesome clothes for it*, Chloe thought with a giggle.

For the first time since arriving at camp, Chloe realized that she was actually a little homesick.

"I thought you just got a new red pair?" Makena said, a hint of envy in her voice. "Those were faboo."

"I did. I guess my mom wanted to get me something for camp," Chloe said, realizing too that she'd never thanked her mom for the gift. The yellow shoes had been sitting on the kitchen counter one morning; she'd just grabbed them as she left for school.

Flavia let out a loud sigh. "OK, girls, are we ready to play?"

"It's hard to control the ball in here," Isa said.

"You're right," Flavia said. "Learning to play on a gym floor will help your ball-handling skills. And it will keep you dry."

On cue, a crash of thunder startled the campers.

"Whoa," Val said. "That was close."

"OK, let us try putting some of those dribbling and ball skills into practice," Flavia said. "You six girls over there and you six girls over here behind the cone. I will feed in the ball. You need to win the ball and pass it to me. First ones to pass can rest. We will play until the last one is left."

"Huh?" Skylar said. Then, in a lower voice, "I can't understand anything she says. It's so annoying."

She nudged Jessie, and the two girls started to snicker.

"Just win the ball," Makena said. "If you can, that is."

Chloe, Val, and Makena were in one group. Luckily, Jessie and Skylar were in the other. Chloe was dying to take on Skylar, but during her first few rounds, she faced other players.

Instead, Makena and Skylar were going at it. The battle to win the ball was borderline wrestling, and Flavia had to blow her whistle so many times that she finally told the girls to switch places in line.

"That's enough," she said with a frown. "Change places."

Chloe was up next. She saw Skylar nudge Jessie out of the way so she could have a turn against Chloe.

"Let's go," Chloe whispered to herself. She had to be quick to the ball and then use her body to shield it until she could get the pass off to Flavia. This was something Coach Lily had spent a lot of time on during Breaker practices. She could hear the coach's voice in her head: *Chloe, use your body to shield the ball until you get your chance. Don't panic, don't do too much, and don't rush.*

She noticed Lars watching from the sidelines and could see Skylar's smug smile from all the way across the field. *She's sure she's going to smoke me*, Chloe thought.

Not today.

"Ready?" Both girls nodded and took their places. "Play!" Flavia yelled and sent the ball onto the court.

Chloe and Skylar sprinted forward as fast as they could. The key was the first touch. Chloe's long legs got her to the ball first, and she touched it lightly away from Skylar, putting herself between Skylar and the ball. Chloe felt a shove from behind but tried to hold her ground. She pulled the ball back with her right foot, trying to get an opening to pass to Flavia. From behind, she felt Skylar hacking at her ankles.

"Hey!" Chloe yelled, expecting to hear Flavia's whistle signaling the foul.

"Come on, Chloe!" Makena called.

"Go, Skylar!" Jessie shouted.

Chloe faked to her right and then turned left, shaking Skylar loose. All she needed to do was get a foot on the ball. Flavia was waiting on the sideline, an impressed look on her face. Chloe was finally beating Skylar one-on-one!

She looked up for an instant and moved to pass the ball with her right foot—when suddenly she felt herself falling hard and slamming onto the gym floor. Skylar's foot blocked the pass...and Flavia's view.

Skylar had Chloe's shirt in her fist.

Chloe lunged forward, but it was no use. Skylar let go of her shirt and leaped over her outstretched leg. She gathered the ball quickly and passed it to Flavia.

The whistle blew. Chloe found herself in a defeated heap on the hard floor.

12

Val's milk bubbles looked like a white sea about to overflow down the sides of her clear plastic cup as she blew harder. At the last second, Val sucked into the straw and brought all the liquid safely back. She smiled at Chloe with lips still sucking and her eyebrows raised as if to say, "How 'bout dat?"

Chloe gave her a weak smile. She could tell Val was doing everything she could to cheer her up after the miserable morning. Makena also was sticking close. They had found a table in a corner far from the rest of the campers. Jessie was off with Skylar somewhere, and Chloe was relieved. She wasn't feeling up to sparring with anyone at the moment.

"You better not spill that all over the place, Val," Makena warned. "I'm done with food issues."

"And sprints," Chloe added. She reached down to massage an aching thigh. *Man, I thought ballet training was hard*, she thought as she worked out a knot in her left leg.

"So I think today is definitely a movie day," Makena said. Afternoon session had been canceled because of the terrible weather. The fields were unplayable, and the younger campers were doing arts and crafts in the indoor space. That was fine with Chloe as she couldn't wait to just run away and curl up in her bunk.

"Yeah, which…" the rest of Val's answer was drowned out by a screech and stampede of girls across the commissary.

"You think…?" Makena stood up suddenly and started to move with the crowd. The only thing that would get this crowd moving like that was either One Direction or the inter-camp roster. Makena stopped to look at Chloe.

"You coming?" she asked, about to break into a run.

"Yeah, I'm coming. Go! Let's go!" Chloe lied.

She watched as Val and Makena rushed off with the rest of the girls and then turned and walked away. *I'm sure they'll tell me who is on the team*, she thought to herself. *I don't need to go running over there.*

Her dorm was about a hundred yards away from the dining hall. She could still hear the girls screeching and chattering on about the team as she waiting under the awning outside the dining hall and watched the rain fall onto the muddy path.

She was about to make her move when the door opened behind her. "It's still pouring," she said, hoping to see Val or Makena.

Instead Skylar stood in the doorway, her head tilted to one side.

"Guess you saw the roster," she said.

Chloe shrugged but didn't answer.

"Don't worry, you can be my water girl."

The door slammed as Skylar laughed and turned back to all the excitement in the commissary. Chloe turned and took off into the rain.

• • •

Chloe thought she heard a light knock on the door but wasn't sure and didn't really care. Water and wind were still shaking the windowpanes. Makena and Val were in the hangout common room watching *Bend It Like Beckham*, one of the girls' favorite soccer movies. They'd tried to cheer her up, but Chloe just said she wanted to be alone. She had decided to read a great book from her summer reading list about a girl who gets lost in Africa. Wrapped up in her blanket, she was hoping the story would take her away for a few hours and fill her mind with anything other than Skylar and rosters.

The tap sounded again. This time she was sure it was real. It couldn't be Makena or Val; they would have just barged in. They had all made the team. Makena, Val, Jessie, Isa, and Skylar. Everyone except Chloe.

"Come in," she called with a sigh.

The door creaked slowly open. Flavia entered, her giant ponytail trailing behind her.

"Chloe, you have a call on the phone downstairs."

"I do?"

"*Si*. It is your mother," Flavia said.

"Oh," Chloe said weakly. *Oh no*, she thought.

"I'll see you in the morning, right?"

"Right."

"I'm sorry you didn't make the team," Flavia said.

Chloe nodded. "It's no biggie," she lied. "See you tomorrow?"

Chloe jumped up from the bed and rushed past Flavia down to the common area. The phone lay on the table, attached to the wall by a long, twisted wire. Chloe had only ever seen a phone connected to the wall in movies.

"Hi, Mom!" she said into the handset, trying to sound

way more chipper than she felt. She could picture her mother on her sleek smartphone, hair perfectly blown out, wearing a tailored suit in a trendy color.

"I'm here too," came her father's voice over the line.

Whoa. Both parents on one call. Chloe didn't think this had ever happened before.

Oh my.

Her father spoke first. "Chloe, we received your email. Please explain yourself."

"Uh. Well, it was no big deal. Uh. Some of the girls had a food fight—"

Her mother interrupted. "You threw food?"

"No, of course not. I didn't throw anything," Chloe answered truthfully. "It's really not a big deal. We all just had to send that email. Everyone in camp did."

There was silence for a minute, and then Chloe detected a faint humming sound.

"Chloe, this is just the sort of thing we were worried about. What sort of girls do they have at this camp anyway? It sounds like *Animal House*."

"What's *Animal House*?" Chloe asked, confused.

"Nothing. Never mind," her father said shortly.

The purring sound continued. *Maybe that's what a landline sounds like*, Chloe thought.

"What's that noise?" she said.

No one answered, but she heard a loud sigh from her mother.

"Well, are you having fun otherwise?" her mother asked. "Are you injured yet?"

Chloe bristled at the *yet*, brushing her fingers against her recently healed eye. "Mom, I'm fine. Camp is so awesome. The girls are great, and I have this amazing coach from Brazil who's teaching me some awesome moves."

"Well, that's good. I hope he's not too hard on you," her mother said, sounding doubtful.

"It's a she, actually. Her name is Flavia, and she's trying to make the Brazilian national team and play in the World Cup!"

"Well, that's nice," her mother said. "But we think maybe you should come home early anyway. It sounds like there's trouble there."

A scuffle and a series of scratching sounds came through the phone.

"It sounds like there's more trouble there than here. What *is* that?" Chloe asked.

In the next instant, she heard soft laughter and recognized her brother's voice, "Hey, Sis, Dad had to hang up. He got attacked by Smitty, who apparently doesn't want him to talk on the phone anymore."

"For heaven's sake," her mother said. "That animal is a tyrant, and your father is ridiculous."

Chloe thought she detected a note of humor in her mother's voice.

"Mom, are you starting to like the cat?" Chloe asked, shocked.

There was silence on the other end. Finally, her mother said, "Well, I wouldn't go that far. But I am enjoying the hassle your father has created for himself. Chloe, take care, please. Madame Olga does not want to see black-and-blue legs."

"OK, Mom, I will," Chloe said, rubbing her eye again.

Things had gone better than she'd feared. This made her suspicious.

"Mom?" she added. She wanted to thank her for the shoes.

No reply.

"She hung up already," Andrew said. "I'm sorry they saw the email. Mom walked by right when I opened it, and I had no idea. She practically pushed me out of the chair. She's been all over that camp website looking for pictures of you, you know."

That didn't sound like her mother. Usually, Chloe felt as if her mother barely had time for her at all.

"She must really hate that I'm here," she said to her brother, trying not to sound sad.

"I'm not sure," Andrew said. "She spent hours researching those new shoes she got you too. The good news is that cat is a total distraction, and Mom won't help Dad take care of him at all. She won't even let Ana clean the litter box. She makes Dad do it."

"Dad cleans the litter box? Are you serious?" Chloe said. Domestic chores were not her father's department.

"Oh yeah, I'll get a picture of it next time. Mind blower for sure. It's become, like, a thing between them. Kind of funny actually. Dad doesn't even seem to mind. Sings while he scoops."

"Dad? Singing and scooping?" Chloe was incredulous.

"I know, right? But the cat is really, really cute, I have to admit. She sleeps a lot, but when Dad comes home, she jumps around like a dog. I think Dad even got Smitty a little leash. That oughta be fun to watch."

Chloe laughed, surprised by how happy she was to hear her family's voices. She was in no hurry to hang up.

"How's the fishing coming?" she asked.

"Pretty good. Still trying to work on my casting." Andrew laughed. "Hey, so how's everyone else doing?"

By "everyone else," Chloe knew he meant Val.

"Everyone's good," she said. "I think everyone might miss you a little bit too."

"Well, tell her I said hi."

"I will," Chloe said. The conversation was winding down, which made her weirdly sad. There was a time, and not long ago, when she and her brother could barely stand to be in the same room. Things really do change sometimes, she thought.

"I'll see you this weekend," Andrew said.

"Yeah, bye."

• • •

The next morning, Chloe made it to her meeting with Flavia nice and early. The storm had passed, and the air was clear, as if all the rain had washed away the humidity and stickiness of the previous days.

Chloe had worn her new indoor shoes to practice with Flavia on the bright green pitch behind the dorms but found herself slipping on the still-wet ground.

"*Bom dia*," Flavia said as she walked up, dribbling a ball. *It is so cool*, Chloe thought, *that a ball is all she ever comes with*. A ball and her feet. Oh, and her giant ponytail. Today, Flavia's hair was in a braid that reached down to her shorts.

"Hi there," Chloe said with a sigh, sitting on a nearby bench.

"You look upset. What's the matter?"

"I wore my new indoor shoes because my new cleats are giving me blisters, but now I keep slipping. It's super annoying."

"I thought you were upset about this team?" Flavia asked.

"Well, yes. But, honestly, I didn't expect to make it anyway," Chloe said.

"Why not?" Flavia asked. "If I had to choose, I would have picked you over many of the other girls."

"Really?" Chloe asked. "But they are way better than I am. They will have a better chance of winning without me."

"That's not all that matters, you know," Flavia answered. "I thought you knew better than that."

Flavia shot Chloe a look, squinting her eye and squishing up her face as if she'd smelled something bad.

"This makes you upset?" Flavia said, waving her arms back and forth, encouraging Chloe to look around. Shaking her head, she grabbed her ball, kicking it against a nearby brick wall. The unevenness of the brick made the ball veer off to the side. Quickly, Flavia chased it down.

"You want to play or no?" she asked without enthusiasm.

"Uh, yeah, yeah, I do," Chloe said, suddenly unsure. She grabbed her ball and hustled over to Flavia. Again, she saw an angry look on her face. It was such a difference from the warm, happy mentor she had come to know.

"Flavia, is something wrong?"

Flavia sighed and shook her head. "No. Let's go."

They started with a short passing warm-up and then moved quickly to one-on-one moves.

Flavia schooled her a few times. Chloe thought she could feel anger emanating from her style of play. Normally, Flavia let her win a few. Not today.

"Are you mad at me, Flavia?" Chloe said. "Because I didn't come yesterday? I'm really sorry."

"No, I am not mad at you—only," Flavia said.

Now Chloe was confused. This had nothing to do with her not showing up yesterday?

"But you *are* mad at me?" Chloe said, alarmed. "And someone else too? Who are you mad at? What did we do?"

"I don't know if I can explain this." Flavia grabbed her ball and walked over to sit on top of the brick wall. "I am angry and sad that you and the other girls don't understand."

"Understand what?" Chloe was close to panicking. Did Flavia think the girls weren't paying attention during training?

"You. All of you complain," Flavia said. "You waste food like it is nothing."

Chloe was at a loss. The food fight was wrong, sure; Lars thought the camp might get in trouble or lose its space to host next year. But this was something else.

"I wore these for you today," Flavia said, pointing at her feet.

Chloe looked down. Flavia's cleats were black with blue stripes. She had two different-colored laces. They seemed regular.

Flavia reached down, taking off her right shoe and handing it to Chloe.

"This. This is what none of you understand," she said.

Chloe took the shoe. It was soft from use. She turned it over and saw that the cleats were worn down almost to the sole of the shoe.

"This is old?" Chloe said tentatively.

Flavia nodded. Taking the shoe back, she turned it over to show Chloe how she'd had to sew the leather back together with needle and thread. Gulping air, Chloe looked down at her brand-spanking-new shoes. She got new cleats practically every season. Fall and spring. Sure, her feet were growing, but really, that was just the way it was. Most of the Breakers bought new shoes whenever they needed them. And, like Chloe, sometimes when they didn't.

Chloe's mind was whirling. She thought about Flavia playing with her brothers as a little girl and having to keep her hair short. She thought about the lack of space Flavia had described in the *favelas*, about never having any privacy.

Then she thought back to her own first soccer team. Someone signed her up. She went to the field. The coaches were waiting. The field was beautiful.

That's just the way it is.

Looking around at the beautiful school grounds, the perfect pitch, Chloe bowed her head and kicked the ground.

"You had to sew your shoes?" she mumbled.

Flavia looked at the shoe in her hand. "All you girls complain if the water is too warm or if you can't win or if the perfect field is not perfect. You have everything right in front of you, but yet you cannot see."

For the rest of that day and evening, Chloe moved around in a daze. Flavia's words hovered over her like a dark storm cloud.

Makena, Val, and the rest of the campers were rehearsing their skits, and Chloe just knew that Jessie and Skylar had something awful planned. Too distracted to focus on Makena and Val's whispered conversation, Chloe watched the other pair from across the room, certain that they were somehow going to find a way to make fun of her.

After a few minutes of whispering and dirty looks, Chloe slipped away. Makena and Val would just tell her what she was supposed to say and do. How hard could it be? For as long as she could remember, she'd been performing onstage for crowds. Even big fancy crowds in New York City and Boston. Get up. Smile. Follow the plan. She didn't think her friends even noticed her leaving.

As Chloe crossed the lush lawn that separated the buildings on her walk back toward the dorms, she felt the soft grass poking up around her flip-flops, tickling her toes. It was close to 10:00 p.m., but the night was bright and clear. Brilliant moonlight flooded through the branches and leaves of the tall oaks, dappling the ground with patches of brightness.

Chloe slowed her steps, enjoying the sounds of summer crickets and rustling leaves. She didn't want to go back to her dorm just yet. Instead, she found a giant tree and plopped down in front of it.

Closing her eyes, she let her thoughts begin to swirl. Flavia's words fell around her like giant drops of pelting rain. That morning, instead of playing any further, they had just talked. Or, rather, Flavia talked and Chloe listened. Flavia shared stories about her life in Brazil, stories of the struggles she and other women faced just trying to play soccer. Chloe had thought all Brazilians loved soccer. It's true, Flavia told her. They do. But it's really for boys, not girls.

In Brookville, playing soccer was just something little kids—girls and boys alike—did when they got to be about six years old. An expected next step. Chloe had had no idea that girls in other places didn't or couldn't do the same thing.

Sighing, Flavia told Chloe the story of Sissi, one of the greatest Brazilian players ever. Only her brothers were given soccer balls to play with. Even to sleep with! Sissi got dolls instead. Finally, she decided to rip the heads off the dolls and kick them around. So her mother at last convinced her father to give her a ball. To save the dolls!

Chloe liked the sound of that girl and smiled at the image of a little kid kicking a doll's head across the field. She wouldn't mind trying that herself.

Were there other places in the world where girls had to fight just to play a game of soccer? Chloe wondered. It had never occurred to her before. She took it for granted that she could do whatever she wanted, whenever she wanted. Her only obstacle was convincing her parents. Imagine having to convince a whole country!

The thought made Chloe feel bone-tired. She slid farther down into the tall, cool grass and admired the moon through the trees, though it was mostly blocked by the canopy of leaves. She rolled over a few times to get a clear view. Soon she was lying in the middle of the green, the night sky above, the moon the color of amber and honey.

She kicked off her shoes and exhaled, allowing her

body to relax for what felt like the first time in weeks. She felt the ground beneath her and was happy to let the solidness of the earth fully support her bones.

She must have dozed off for a moment. She awoke suddenly, startled to feel something brushing against her feet.

"Dude? Are you dead?" a small voice asked. It was Val, of course.

And Makena. "Where'd you go?" Makena said. "Why are you lying in the middle of the grass?"

"I like it," Chloe said.

"You like it?" Makena said. "OK then."

She plopped down on the grass next to Chloe.

Val shrugged her shoulders, said, "OK, dudes," and settled down next to them.

Chloe smiled.

"So we made up the skit," Makena said. "It's pretty funny, if I do say so myself."

"Awesome. Tell me my part later?" Chloe said.

There was a moment of silence.

"You OK?" Val said. "Are you still upset about not making the team?"

Chloe shook her head, enjoying the rustling of the grass around her ears. "I was," she admitted. "But not so much anymore."

"Are you having deep thoughts or something?" Makena asked.

Chloe smiled, inhaling the sweet summer air. "I guess I am."

"Don't hurt yourself," Makena said and burst into a fit of laughter. "Hey, want to put your head on my stomach, and then we'll all laugh and then laugh harder because we're all already laughing?"

Chloe grinned, looking up at Makena, and shook her head. "Maybe in a minute."

She saw Makena's puzzled look but closed her eyes anyway. Her mind was starting to drift when she heard the terrible *smack* of hand hitting skin.

"Gotcha!" Makena yelped, wiping remnants of dead mosquito off on the grass. "Ugh, I have so many bites. I look like I have chicken pox."

"You know, you can rub a banana peel on a mosquito bite, and it takes away the swelling," Val said.

"What? That's the dumbest thing I ever heard," Makena said. "Who told you that?"

"Um, your mother," Val said with a giggle.

Makena rolled her eyes and lay back down on the grass.

"And did you know that only female mosquitos bite humans? The males just eat flower nectar."

Makena covered her face with her hands. "Fascinating," she said with a sigh. "And let me guess who told you that?"

"Your mother!" Chloe and Val answered together.

Makena kept her face covered, but Chloe could see from the crinkle of her eyes that she was smiling. Her mom was one of the world's foremost insect experts. Day in and day out, Makena heard a lot about bugs.

"Your mom's really smart, Makena," Chloe said. "You should listen to her sometimes."

"Oh, yeah? Like you listen to yours!" Makena said.

"Good point," Chloe said with a nod. *Maybe I should try that*, she thought.

Abruptly, Val sat up and turned to Chloe. "You know, when I first met you, I thought you would be really different."

"Yeah, you certainly didn't know she had such a cute brother!" Makena teased.

Val jumped up and piled on top of Makena. "Will you shut up!" she squealed, trying to put her hand across Makena's mouth.

Then, sitting on top of Makena, Val turned again to Chloe. "I'm serious. I thought you would be totally stuck up or something."

Makena squirmed to free herself as Val spoke. Giggling, Val kept holding her down.

Chloe laughed, "Stuck up?"

"Dude, you have everything! You're the most popular girl around!" Val said.

"Oh, please. I'm not too popular at this camp," Chloe said, surprised that she was able to admit the truth to her friends so freely.

The girls fell quiet. Sighing, Val rolled off Makena and lay on the grass next to her.

"I wish Skylar hadn't come," Makena said. "She ruins everything. Don't you think?"

Chloe thought about all the taunts and mean comments she'd had to endure during the weeks of camp. But somehow she couldn't bring herself to agree with Makena.

"Here, let's lie down head to toe," Val suggested. "We can form a triangle. You know, soccer is all about triangles!"

Chloe and Makena shifted to form the shape. Val gave Chloe's head a little tap with her foot, but Chloe didn't move away. She wouldn't let many people put their toes near her nose, but she loved feeling connected to her girls. She nestled her foot in the crook of Makena's shoulder. Instead of moving away, Makena tilted her head and rested her face on Chloe's ankle.

The three girls lay on the grass, heads and feet touching, staring up at the summer sky. *Why do I feel so connected to my Soccer Sisters?* Chloe wondered. It wasn't just that they all loved the same sport. It was something else, something deeper.

She thought about Flavia as a little girl, cutting her hair to be able to play soccer. And Sissi, the star that ripped her dolls' heads off so she could join in the game. Chloe didn't know Sissi and probably never would, but somehow she felt like she did. Why was that?

She thought about fierce Val and zany Makena and even Skylar, cruel as she was. They were all unique. From different cultures and places yet still somehow similar on the inside.

Suddenly, she knew what they shared.

Determination.

They didn't give up, and neither would she.

"This is what I think. I think that even with Skylar here, we are really, really lucky."

C hloe's embrace of luck and friendship lasted through the first few skits. There were Lars impersonations, including Lauren wearing a giant white mop on her head, running around the room shouting "Alrighty then!" and counting in Dutch. There was a mime routine about penalty kicks that completely freaked Makena out. Still, Chloe enjoyed watching the campers try to entertain one another.

When there was an unusually long pause between skits though, Chloe noticed people sneaking looks at her. She knew some of the girls still blamed her for the food fight sprints, but for the most part, camp life was so full and moved so fast that the incident had mostly been forgotten.

Or so she thought.

More girls were looking at Chloe now. She was sure of it. It was as if they were expecting something, but she had no idea what.

The nice girl named Isa jumped onstage. She wore a green Mexico jersey and looked kind of uncomfortable. She held a soccer ball under her right arm.

Then Jessie showed up. She was in a yellow Brazil jersey and had several long, black pieces of rope hanging down her back.

It didn't take long to figure out that Jessie was supposed to be Flavia, and the rope was meant to imitate their coach's long ponytail.

Chloe and Val shared a look.

Was Isa supposed to be Val?

Then Skylar came out.

Chloe sucked in her breath, afraid she might throw up. She watched in horror as Skylar waltzed onto the stage carrying a large brown bag.

She looked at Val, who just shook her head.

Chloe felt Makena grab her hand and whisper, "It's OK." But Chloe knew it wasn't. She closed her eyes, but she couldn't get the image out of her head. She should have known. Slowly, she opened her eyes and watched as Skylar spun around. On her toes.

Wearing a giant pink tutu.

Some campers laughed hysterically, many of them pointing at Chloe. Val and Makena moved closer, as if to create a protective friend force field.

But there was no protection from this attack.

Skylar pranced around the stage for a few more minutes and then came to a stop in front of Jessie and Isa.

"*Hola*," Jessie said in a terrible accent that sounded nothing like the Spanish word for "hello."

"*Hola*, dude," Isa said back, looking uncomfortable. Beside her, Chloe felt Val tense.

"Let's play," Jessie said, pretending to be Flavia leading a drill.

Skylar danced in between Jessie and Isa, spinning around and yelling, "Wheeeee, look at meeee! I'm sooo perfect and pretttty!"

Some of the laughter died away as Skylar continued to dance.

Chloe caught Flavia's eye from the across the room. The coach shook her head and looked at the floor.

Skylar motioned for Isa to give her something, but Isa shook her head. The girl was frozen, looking around at the horrified coaches and campers in the audience.

Frustrated, Skylar rushed over to Isa and grabbed

the ball out of her hands. She tossed it on the ground and danced over to it.

"Oh, Flavia, please help me!" she whined.

No one was laughing anymore at this ugly and pointless skit. No one except Skylar. Chloe could see Lars making his way to the front of the stage. His eyes were narrowed with fury.

"Oh, take this!" she said and reached into the brown bag, which contained pieces of bread and grapes. Skylar grabbed the food and started to chuck it at Jessie and Isa. Then she turned and tossed the rest into the crowd.

"Alrighty then!" Lars bounded onto the stage and grabbed the bag. "That's enough." He held his arm out until Skylar reluctantly handed him the tutu. With a disgusted look, he turned to the crowd and asked, "Who's next?"

Chloe felt a nudge from Makena on her right. To her left, she saw Val getting up. Makena nodded her head.

"You have got to be kidding," Chloe whispered. They were next?

All eyes in the room were on her. Every camper present knew that Skylar had thrown down the gauntlet. Or the tutu, as the case might be.

"You going to let her get away with that?" a voice said.

Chloe turned to see the same young girl who'd questioned her after the food fight.

"You again," Chloe said with a shake of her head.

"Well, are you? You just going to take that?" The girl tilted her head in Skylar's direction. "Come on. We all know she's the problem child."

Chloe didn't know how to respond. She felt Makena pulling her by the arm.

"Let's get this over with," Makena said.

The room was silent as Makena, Val, and Chloe gathered backstage. Through the gap in the curtains, Chloe saw Flavia looking around. She seemed to be searching the stage for someone, her eyes narrow and focused.

Chloe was nearly shaking with anxiety. The skit Makena and Val had come up with was simple and kind of silly actually. Makena, as the host of a fake TV show called *Soccer Talk*, would interview her "guests," Val and Chloe. Chloe hadn't practiced at all, and she barely knew her part.

Now all eyes were on her.

Was she just going to take that?

"Welcome to *Soccer Talk*!" Makena said, giving a big wave of her hands. She'd put a T-shirt on her head that made her look like she had long orange hair. Now she pulled up a folding chair with a flourish and brushed it off, earning a few chuckles. "This is the most important show on the twenty-four-hour soccer network, Super Soccer Stuff! My name is Lola Von Futbol…and I'd like to introduce my first guest…Lionel Messi!"

That got the campers' attention. They all cheered as Val took the stage in an Argentina jersey, dribbling the ball with her left foot. When the ball moved to her right foot, she ran around it so she could touch it only with her left. This got a good laugh from the crowd: Messi was perhaps the greatest current player in the world, but he was pretty one-footed. Soccer players had to be able to use both feet, but kids everywhere loved to frustrate their coaches by pointing out that Messi's right foot was nothing compared to his left.

"*Hola! Yo soy* Lionel Messi!" Val said, introducing herself in perfect Spanish.

Makena used her hands to make a pretend microphone, "Now, we all know Mr. Messi is one of the greatest players in the world! But what you probably don't know is that he also has a side job as a comedian!"

Gasps sounded from the crowd. "It's true, soccer people!" Makena assured them.

"Oh *si*," Val said in a funny voice. "Tell me, Lola Von Futbol, why did Cinderella get kicked off the soccer team?"

"I don't know, Mr. Messi. Why did Cinderella get kicked off the soccer team?"

"Because she ran away from the ball!"

There were boos and hisses from the crowd. But a few chuckles as well.

"Tell me, Mr. Messi, how did the field get all wet?" Makena asked, trying to save the skit.

"Ah," Val said, "How did the field get all wet? Well, the players dribbled all over it, of course!" Chloe watched the crowd's reaction. There were a few chuckles, but while the skit was cute, it was falling flat.

Chloe was the next guest on *Soccer Talk*. *Oh no*, she thought. *This is bad enough already.* She did not want to get up on that stage. She could hardly remember what Makena and Val had told her to say. She was supposed to be Alex Morgan, who was actually a secret magician or something dumb like that.

Desperately, Chloe looked to the side of the stage for the deck of cards. She just had to do one card trick, and then this awful skit night would be over.

Again, she peered out into the crowd, taking in all the faces. An unusual feeling filled her stomach. Chloe had performed to sold-out crowds before. She'd never felt nervous, not ever. How could she have stage fright over a soccer camp skit?

Her eyes drifted to the back of the room. There was Skylar. She had a triumphant look on her face, and Chloe knew the other girl was just waiting for her to get onstage so she could mock her. If she'd learned anything this week, it was that Skylar didn't care what Lars or anyone else said or thought. She could be relentless in her cruelty.

Why? Chloe wondered. *What is it about me that makes her want to pick on me?*

Chloe looked again for the deck of cards, but she couldn't see them. Something pink and frilly caught her eye. The tutu. Chloe leaned down to pick it up. It was made of stiff, rough fabric that felt more like fishing net. She shook her head; she hadn't worn a tutu like this since she was about three years old. Now her costumes were crafted of soft, flowing organza that kissed her skin as she twirled. If only Skylar could see what Chloe was really capable of, she wouldn't make fun of it anymore.

Chloe stopped in her tracks.

She rubbed the fabric between her fingers.

She knew exactly what to do.

15

ionel Messi, thank you very much!" Chloe heard Makena say in her fake television host voice. "My next guest is the fabulous Alex Morgan!"

Chloe heard a smattering of applause from behind the makeshift curtain. The clapping was, of course, for the real Alex Morgan, U.S. National Team superstar and idol to nearly every girl at camp.

Chloe took a deep breath, like she did before every big performance. It was hard to imagine having more nerves over a soccer camp skit than at Lincoln Center. Val bounded by with a smile and a whispered "Good luck!"

Squaring her shoulders, Chloe adjusted her tutu and walked onto the stage.

Makena's eyes practically bugged out of her head. The

tutu was certainly not part of the plan, but Chloe saw Makena shrug as if to say, "OK, I'll go with it."

"It's a great honor to have Alex Morgan with us this evening!" Makena, as Lola, said. "Welcome to *Soccer Talk*!"

"Oh, wow, it's great to be here," Chloe said in a slow surfer-girl accent. Alex Morgan was a California girl through and through.

"Uh, Alex," Makena said, clearly figuring things out on the fly. "I see that you have on a special outfit this evening. Is this a new interest of yours?"

"Oh, yeah, and I'm so glad you asked," Chloe said. "See, since I'm just excellent at everything I do, I recently decided to become a ballerina."

After Skylar's cruel skit mocking her dancing, Chloe knew that all the campers' eyes would be glued to her next move.

She wasn't going to disappoint.

Without another word, Chloe stood on her toes, in as perfect a pointe as she could manage. Then she performed a *grand battement* in which her leg reached up nearly behind her head. The stunned gasps from the crowd thrilled her. Grinning, she launched into seven *fouettés en tournant*, moves that required incredible balance and coordination, using the whipping motion of her leg to spin herself around.

When she finished the last turn, head held high, she caught the eye of Bella, the little girl who had questioned her so strongly. The young camper was staring at Chloe in awe, mouth agape, eyes bright with admiration. Chloe gave her a wink. She didn't see Skylar watching, but she could feel all eyes upon her.

"Wow! Chloe! I…er…I mean, Alex, that was something else!" Makena said from the hostess chair. Chloe could tell she was impressed too. The truth was none of her soccer friends had ever seen what she was capable of when it came to dance. When she thought about it, Chloe realized, she'd been hiding it from them. She just wasn't sure why.

"So does this mean you will be giving up soccer, Alex?" Makena continued.

"Oh no, not at all," Chloe said. She nodded at Val offstage, asking for a ball. "I'll never give up soccer," she added with more force than she'd intended.

Grabbing the ball, she dropped it to her right foot and began to juggle. First with only her right foot and then only her left. She used her thighs and every so often her head.

She could hear the sighs from the girls on the floor when she did a neck stall, in which she basically caught the ball on the back of her neck and held it, poised.

Bella let out a yelp of joy. Chloe smiled and decided in an instant to try her most difficult freestyle trick, the Around the World. She had to do a single revolution around the ball with her foot and then continue juggling. If the ball hit the ground at any point, it wouldn't count.

Chloe kept the ball going until she was ready. She didn't dare look up to see if Skylar was watching. But she was certain she was. Everyone was.

Bella was clapping now with every touch of the ball, giddy with admiration.

Chloe was ready. She'd only managed to do a few perfect Around the Worlds, but she knew she would shut Skylar up once and for all if the move was clean.

She set the ball up perfectly and managed to complete the revolution with ease. She decided to catch the ball on her foot and rest for a minute, maybe check out Skylar's expression.

As Bella cheered and the ball settled on her foot, a movement to the side caught her attention. Chloe did a double take, feeling a rush of joy sweep through her body. Was that really her brother standing in the corner? Was it Andrew's boyish grin beaming at her from across the room? How could he be here?

A head popped up beside Andrew's, as if the person had

bent over and scooped something up off the ground. Was that…her father? Was he holding something in his arms?

OMG. OMG. OMG.

If her brother and father were here, that could only mean one thing.

Chloe's mother was here too!

Chloe felt herself wobble. The ball started to slip off her foot. She couldn't let it hit the floor; if she did, Skylar would never let her hear the end of it.

Why in the world was her mother here? Chloe tried to focus, but she felt her concentration slipping away. She just had to finish her freestyle without making a mistake, she told herself. That's all she wanted to do.

Twisting agilely, she managed to get the ball back onto the middle of her foot. Now all she needed to do was flick it up into the air and catch it.

She saw her then, out of the corner of her eye. Her mother, in the back of the room, her eyes fixed on the stage.

Chloe's juggles became chaotic. She started to lose control. Her right foot tapped the ball way too hard, and it flew across the stage. There was no way she could reach it in time. She moved to follow its path, trying to speed over before it hit the ground. In the crowd, she heard Bella gasp.

Even moving as quickly as she could, Chloe knew it

was hopeless. The ball was going to bounce off the stage and into the crowd, leaving her vulnerable to Skylar yet again. Worst of all, it was happening in front of her mother. Chloe watched in despair as the ball began to fall. Her head began to drop along with it.

But the ball never connected with the stage. Instead, it found another foot. A foot wearing a shoe that had been sewn together many times.

Flavia. Flavia was onstage too, and she had caught the ball on her own foot. With a grin, she flicked it back to Chloe. The two girls began to pass the ball back and forth in the air. As it passed between them, a rhythm began.

A beautiful dance, Chloe thought to herself with a smile.

All of sudden, Makena bounded between them and caught the ball.

"Alex Morgan, everyone!" she shouted, and the crowd erupted into cheers. "Thank you, Alex! You have shown us all how truly talented you are."

Chloe beamed at Makena and then turned to the screaming crowd. Skylar wasn't clapping, but she gave Chloe a small nod. It wasn't friendship, but maybe it was a touch of respect.

"Yeah!" Andrew was yelling the loudest. Flavia

came and put her arm around Chloe, who was searching the crowd.

When she found her mother's eyes, she saw it. Finally. Pride.

The referee's whistle blew to signal the end of the first half, and the girls started moving toward the sanctuary of the bench and a breather. It was a hot and humid summer afternoon, and the game had been tough so far.

"Let's go, girls!" Lars called to them. "Come on in! Heads up, everyone!"

"That girl totally stepped on me!" Makena complained as she reached the water cooler. "Did you see that? Jeez, I thought this was supposed to be a 'friendly match' between camps."

"There's no such thing as 'friendly' in soccer, dude," Val said. "You know that!"

Chloe and the rest of the girls nodded. She was right, of course. It had been an intense but scoreless first forty-five minutes with lots of pushing and shoving.

"Makena, get some water, and then we will talk," Flavia said, urging the girls toward the shade of a nearby tree. Chloe thought she detected a trickle of mischief in her voice.

Makena broke into a grin and seemed to momentarily forget her frustration. Chloe turned away to stifle a laugh.

"Let's all get some water, shall we?" Val said with a smirk.

Chloe, Makena, and Val turned together and grabbed a cup of ice-cold water from an orange plastic tray. A tray held by none other than the infamous Skylar. Next to her stood Jessie with a bag full of orange slices. Both Skylar and Jessie had fake smiles plastered on their faces, their eyes betraying their humiliation.

"Oh, I love oranges, don't you?" Chloe said, taking a small bite.

"Yesh," Makena said with a nod, stuffing an entire orange quarter in her mouth. "Nith n juithy."

Chloe laughed and backed away. Lars and Flavia were total geniuses. They had come up with the perfect punishment for Skylar and Jessie's outrageous and ignorant skit. First, they were benched for the big game, but better than that, they were not sent home early. Instead, they were required to stay and provide the players with water, oranges, towels, and whatever else they needed. Chloe thought making them suffer through the game was pure brilliance. Justice. Had they just been sent home, they could have made up some excuse as to why they didn't get to play.

It seemed Chloe was not alone in thinking they deserved it. Even Skylar's and Jessie's parents seemed to support the punishment. Chloe stole a glance to her right to see both their dads hovering nearby with stern looks and crossed arms, which was good because Chloe was sure Skylar was dying to dump the whole tray right on her and her friends' heads.

But the best outcome by far was that without Jessie and Skylar on the roster, Lars needed another player and gave Chloe the nod.

Chloe was still relishing Flavia's visit to break the news the night before. Chloe had been packing and showing her mother around the dorms.

"You've earned it, Chloe," Flavia had said. "Lars was very impressed by your juggling tonight."

"So was I, Chloe," her mother added.

"Thanks. I've been practicing a lot!"

Flavia handed Chloe the coveted blue uniform, smiled, and left.

Jenna Gordon tilted her head to the side and seemed to be studying her daughter. "You look pretty happy," she said.

"I am, Mom," Chloe answered with a nod. "And see? All in one piece."

Chloe stuck out her leg, pointed her toes, lifted her leg high into the air, and held it in her arm.

Her mother laughed. "I see that."

"Mom, thanks for letting me come to camp."

Chloe slowly lowered her leg, performed a little pirouette, and ended with a dramatic and graceful bow. She felt strong and prouder than she had in a long time.

"Like a beautiful swan," her mother said. Then, looking down at her daughter's feet, she shook her head and added, "In cleats!"

Chloe hugged her mother for what felt like a long time and over her shoulder caught Val and Makena gesturing for Chloe to join them and pointing and making faces at her.

"These are my sisters, Mom."

"I know that now," her mother answered. Together they turned to see Val and Makena gesturing wildly. They were pointing at her mother and then to the other side of the field. Chloe looked to see Lars standing expectantly, hands on hips. Startled, Chloe realized that her mom was so clueless about soccer she didn't even know she wasn't allowed to be with the team until the game was over.

Lars's booming instruction snapped her back into the moment.

"Ahem, if we can ask all to watch from the other side of the field for the rest of the game, please."

Jenna Gordon took the hint. "Go get 'em, girls!" she said as she moved to the other side of the field with the rest of the parents.

Lars waited a beat as the girls giggled and then began his halftime talk.

"Makena, don't worry about the girl who fouled you. Play your game. Don't let them distract you. Only think about what you can control; don't worry about what you cannot control."

Makena looked unconvinced but seemed to be listening closely to Lars's advice. Suddenly, Chloe felt Flavia pull her over to the side.

"Listen, Goose, the girl on the right defense is slow. You can beat her," she said.

Chloe saw the girl in her mind. She was tough, but Flavia was right. The defender was hesitant to move up when her team was attacking. But Chloe knew she had also been holding back.

"OK," she said. "Which move?"

Flavia looked at her for a moment. She pursed her lips before she responded.

"I cannot tell you which move to make. This is your dance, remember? You know what to do. Last night, you just followed the ball and used your skill, and you were better than anyone thought. Even better than you thought you could be. No?"

Chloe smiled and nodded. She could do it. She knew it. Suddenly, she reached for Flavia and hugged her tight.

"Thank you, Flavia," she said. "Thank you for teaching me so much. And not just about soccer."

Flavia pulled Chloe back by the shoulders, the coach's warm brown eyes rimmed with tears.

"I'm going to miss you, Chloe. I'll remember you when I am playing back home."

Flavia was leaving for Brazil the very next day. She was going to train with a professional team outside of São Paulo and then try out for the Brazilian National Team. The image of the little girl with the short hair flashed before Chloe's eyes.

"I know you'll make it," Chloe said. "You just have to. Then maybe you can come to visit me!"

Flavia shook her head. "No. You are the one who

must come to visit me. The little girls of Brazil would love your moves."

"That would be so, so, so…amazing," Chloe said.

Suddenly, she felt a poke in the side.

"What the heck is going on here?" Makena asked. "Are we going to play some soccer or what?"

Chloe and Flavia laughed. Makena was on a mission.

"Where's Val?" Makena demanded. No mission was complete without her sidekick. Chloe looked around and quickly found Val off to the side and deep in conversation with Andrew. She pointed.

Val flipped her short hair a little in a move that made Makena roll her eyes in disgust. "Ugh. I'll be right back."

Chloe giggled as Makena trotted over to Val and grabbed Val's hand. She didn't say anything at first but just gently pulled, like a ranch hand leading a reluctant horse.

"OK, lovebirds, we've got some soccer yet to play, OK?" Makena muttered as she brought Val back to the team huddle.

"Dude, you're embarrassing me!" Val said, her face flushed crimson. But she was also grinning from ear to ear. Chloe gave her brother a shrug and a smile. Those two were darn cute, she had to admit.

Again, the whistle blew, calling the teams back to

the beautiful field. Chloe jogged into position. She stole a glance at her mom, who gave a wave, a big smile, and even a small cheer.

Wow. Chloe never thought she'd see that!

Movement at the circle caught her attention. The other team was about to kick off.

She could hear Lars's booming voice from the sidelines. "Right away, girls! On the ball!" Stress and urgency coated his voice. *He really wants this*, Chloe thought.

A trickle of sweat dripped down her cheek. Liquid anticipation.

She realized she really wanted it too.

Chloe peered downfield and spotted the girl who had been covering her all game. She was tall, fit, and fierce. All in all a skilled and tough defender. But, of course, Flavia was right: she wasn't as quick as Chloe.

The whistle sounded, and the other team made a critical mistake: dribbling right into the path of Makena and Val. Val pounced and Makena followed, stealing the ball from the startled striker.

Chloe got herself out wide to the left. She wanted the space so when she got the ball she could move up the line and build up speed.

"Mac!" Chloe called, clapping her hands together

quickly to indicate she was ready to receive a pass. "To space!"

Makena looked up and then floated a perfect pass. Chloe moved forward to meet the ball as it gently descended. Chloe gathered the ball with her left foot and pushed quickly ahead. The wind rushed through her ears, competing with the rising cheers. She lifted her head as she dribbled quickly downfield, encouraged by her coaches and parents.

She heard one voice above the din. "Beat her, Goose, beat her!"

The defender approached, trying to cut Chloe off. She was poised like a cat ready to pounce. Chloe slowed her dribble, knowing that the key was her change of pace. She would speed up again once she made her move.

But what move would she make? A step over? A pull back? Would she burst past the defender at just the right time?

Even as she flew down the field, time seemed to slow.

Faces from the last difficult week replayed in Chloe's mind. Makena and Val. Skylar and Jessie. Flavia. Her mother. Each image a reminder of all she had experienced. Friendship. Betrayal. Defeat. Inspiration.

A sudden lunge from the defender brought her back. Now. This was it.

Chloe deftly lifted her left leg in a sweeping circle to the outside, exactly the direction the defender wanted her to go. But it was just a fake. Her foot swept over the ball, and the defender shifted her weight hard to the left.

Quick and sharp, Chloe used her right foot to push the ball to the side and propelled her body forward. She moved past the defender and was just about free when she felt an arm grabbing at her shirt.

The fight wasn't over yet.

Chloe lurched her upper body forward, trying to shake the girl off. The ball floated just in front of her.

Chloe felt her momentum starting to ebb. She was losing her speed.

A second defender was closing in.

I will not quit, Chloe said to herself.

Determination and willpower flowed through her as she gathered her remaining strength. *I can do this. I can. I can beat her one-on-one.*

With a final push forward, she felt the hand, and her doubts, fall away.

Chloe ran free.

Soccer Sisters Team Code

1. Team first.
2. Don't be a poor sport or loser.
3. Play with each other and don't take the fun out of it.
4. Never put someone down if they make a mistake.
5. Practice makes perfect.
6. Never give up on the field or on one another.
7. Leave it on the field.
8. Always do the right thing.
9. Bring snacks on assigned days.
10. Beat the boys at recess soccer.

Book Club Questions and Activities

1. What was the most important lesson Chloe learned and how did she learn it?

2. What makes someone a bully?

3. What made Jessie break from her Soccer Sisters and become close with Skylar?

4. Was the food fight punishment appropriate? Why or why not?

5. Why was Flavia particularly upset when Chloe bailed on their morning practice session?

6. How you do think Flavia felt being a coach at such a privileged camp?

7. Why did Chloe feel more comfortable confiding in her brother? Do you have siblings that you confide in?

8. Why did Chloe's mother want her to excel in ballet so much? What do you think it was about soccer that made her less enthusiastic about it?

9. Chloe seemed uninterested in ballet camp at the beginning of the book but was proud of her skills by the end. What changed?

10. How did Chloe's mother change over the course of the book? Do you think she supported Chloe's love of soccer by the end? Why or why not?

11. Chloe and Flavia came from very different backgrounds. But what experiences made them similar?

12. Why did Flavia save the day onstage when Chloe lost focus juggling?

13. Do you think Skylar learned a lesson after Chloe's skit? What was the lesson?

Women's Soccer in Brazil
by Kely Nascimento-DeLuca

Without a doubt, Brazil is known as *the* soccer country. Brazilians love their *futebol* so much that a great player is often thought of as a hero, and young boys who show a talent for the sport are a great source of pride for their families.

The South American nation has produced a number of talented players—I would bet that most people who are even remotely soccer-aware could name at least two or three Brazilian players. Neymar may be one; Ronaldinho or Kaká might be others. And of course almost everyone knows the name Pelé. He is considered by many to be the greatest player who ever lived.

But did you know that Pelé is not the only Brazilian soccer player considered to be the best in the world? There's another player you may not have heard much about, and her name is Marta.

Marta Vieira da Silva was born in the state of Alagoas in 1986. She has won two Olympic Silver medals with the

Brazilian National Team, and FIFA (Federation Internacional de Football Association), the governing body of international football, awarded her five Ballon d'Or prizes in five consecutive years. The Ballon d'Or is given to the player that FIFA decides is the MVP of *all* that year's European tournaments. Unfortunately, not many people know Marta, and even fewer—soccer lovers included—can name other great women players from Brazil, though there are many.

The truth is that if you're a young Brazilian girl who loves to play soccer, your future looks very different than it would if you were a boy. Many parents don't want their daughters to play because they consider it dangerous and too rough. They don't want their girls to get hurt or have scars when they grow up. Girls are often bullied for wanting to play, and it doesn't help that most neighborhoods don't have all-girls teams, so they often end up playing on boys teams.

Parents also know there are simply fewer opportunities for girls who play soccer, because there is no way you can earn a living as a female soccer player in Brazil. All-women teams are considered amateur teams, so even those playing in a league need a "real" or second job to earn enough money to pay rent and buy food.

It should be said that Brazil is not alone. Most countries don't consider women's soccer a profession. But the great news is that this is changing. For the finals of the 2015 Women's World Cup, 750 million viewers tuned in to watch the U.S. beat Japan. These record numbers are showing the world a few things we already know: Girls are *amazing*. Girls can do *anything*. A girl with a dream is unstoppable. Women's soccer is here to stay!

So please keep playing, keep watching, and make your voices heard!

If you would like to know more about organizations that use soccer to empower girls in Brazil and all over the world, here are some sites you can visit:

guerreirasproject.com

goalsarmenia.com

womenwin.org

equalplayingfield.com/#hike

streetfootballworld.org/project/levelling-playing-field

acerbrasil.org.br/

ACER Brasil is an organization working in Diadema—a "favela" outside of São Paulo. They use sports, dance, language, art, and music to teach children and reduce inequalities in the community.

Kely Nascimento-DeLuca is the daughter of soccer legend Pclé (Edson Arantes do Nascimento) and is currently working on a documentary on women's soccer in Brazil.

Meet Our Soccer Sisters Ambassador Brandi Chastain!

Brandi Chastain—NCAA, World Cup, and Olympic icon—is best known for her game-winning penalty kick against China in the 1999 FIFA Women's World Cup final. She also played on the teams that won the inaugural Women's World Cup in 1991, Olympic gold medals in 1996 and 2004, and the country's first professional women's league championship.

Chastain is the executive director and a head coach of the California Thorns. She is also currently the coach of the Bellarmine College Preparatory varsity boys' soccer team and was a color commentator on soccer telecasts for NBC and ABC/ESPN. In addition, Chastain is an active advocate for several causes that are important to her, including safe play and education about concussion injuries, Crohn's disease and awareness of the illness especially in young children, and equal rights for women in sports.

Brandi is married to Jerry Smith, who is the women's soccer coach at her alma mater, Santa Clara University. She has one son, Jaden, and is also a volunteer assistant coach at Santa Clara.

Soccer Sisters Organization

Soccer Sisters aims to inspire and connect young girls and women through sports-based stories and experiences.

We are a social enterprise aimed at reaching sports-oriented young kids and women with inspiring experiences that give back. Our first set of products is the Soccer Sisters book series for middle grade children:

Out of Bounds
Caught Offside
One on One

To learn more about Soccer Sisters, please visit our website and our social handles:

soccersisters.com

Instagram @soccersisters.forever
facebook.com/soccersisters
Twitter @soccersisters

Part of being a Soccer Sister is giving back. Here are some great groups that are supporting soccer and girls all over the world. Check them out!

coachesacrosscontinents.org
Coaches Across Continents is a global leader in the sport for social impact movement.

goalsarmenia.org
Girls of Armenia Leadership Soccer (GOALS) empowers girls throughout the communities of Armenia, using soccer as a vehicle for change and opportunity.

oneworldplayproject.com
One World Play Project encourages the power of play all over the world.

ussoccerfoundation.org
The U.S. Soccer Foundation helps foster an active

and healthy lifestyle, using soccer to cultivate critical life skills that pave the path to a better future.

fifa.com/womens-football/live-your-goals/index.html
FIFA inspires women and girls to play soccer and stay in the game.

goalsforgirls.org
Goals for Girls uses soccer to teach young women life skills on how to be agents of change in their own lives and in their communities.

Soccer Sisters Roster

BROOKVILLE BREAKERS

Makena Walsh

Valentina Flores

Chloe Gordon

Jessie Palise

Ariana Murray

Harper Jones

Sydney Lin

Abby Rosen

Tessa Jordan

Kat Emelin

Ella Devine

Jasmine Manikas

Coach Lily James

Glossary

50/50 ball: When a player from each team tries to win a loose ball (and they each have a 50/50 chance of doing so).

Assist: When a player gets the ball to a second player, who scores as a result of the pass.

Bench: Where the substitutes sit during the game.

Box: The box that is formed when a line is drawn eighteen yards out from each goalpost along the goal line. The lines extend eighteen yards into the field of play and are connected with a line that is parallel to the goal line.

Breakaway: When an offensive player is going to goal with the ball and has left all defenders behind. A rare and very exciting event!

Captain: The player or players who have been designated by the coach or team to lead and represent the team during a game. The captain is the only player allowed to speak to the referee. A captain is often given a distinctive armband.

Caution: When the referee shows a yellow card to a player after a foul. It's a warning or "caution" to calm down and play by the rules. A player given two yellow cards in one game is ejected from the field! You don't want to get yellow cards.

Center circle: A circle with a ten-yard radius, drawn with the center mark as its center.

Clear: A term used by defenders to send the ball rapidly upfield. This term is yelled out by defenders to alert the defender with the ball that she has impending pressure.

Cleats: Shoes worn by soccer players. So called for the studs or cleats on the soles of the shoes that help grip the grass and prevent slipping.

Corner kick: A kick awarded to the attacking team when the ball, having last been touched by the defending team, crosses the goal line and goes out of bounds. The ball is placed in the corner, duh!

Cross: A ball that has been kicked or thrown (from a throw-in) from near the touch line toward the goal.

Crossbar: The structure of the goal that connects the two upright goalposts.

Dead ball situation: Any situation when the ball is put back into play. Sounds creepy but isn't.

Dive: When a player fakes being fouled and falls to the ground. Unfortunately, it happens all the time.

Dribble: Moving the ball forward with the feet (similar to basketball but with your feet!).

Far post: The goalpost that is farthest from the ball.

Forward: An offensive player playing closest to the opponent's goal.

Foul: An offense against an opponent or against the spirit of the game that results in a free kick.

Free kick: A method of restarting play.

Give-and-go: Just what it sounds like: A player passes to a teammate, runs, and gets the ball back from the same teammate. You "give" the ball, and then you "go."

Goal: 1. The structure defined by two upright goalposts and one crossbar that is set on the goal line. 2. To score.

Goal kick: A kick awarded to the defensive team after the attacking team has put the ball over the defending team's goal line. Opposite of a corner kick, the ball is placed close to the goal. Duh number two.

Golden goal: The goal in "sudden victory" overtime that wins and ends the game.

Hand ball: When a player, not the goalie, touches the ball with a hand or part of the arm.

Header: Passing, clearing, controlling, or shooting the ball with the head. This has recently been outlawed for younger kids to prevent collisions and concussions.

Juggling: A practice skill when the ball is kept in the air using any legal part of the body.

Keep-away: A practice game where the object is for one side to retain possession rather than to score goals.

Near post: The goalpost that is nearest to the ball.

Nutmeg: When a player puts the ball through the legs of an opposing player, a player is said to have been "nutmegged" or "megged." Don't let this happen to you!

Offside: A player is called "offside" when she is nearer to her opponent's goal than both the ball and the second-last opponent. It's confusing for many parents and sometimes players and referees!

Own goal: A goal scored by a player into her own team's net. Very sad event.

Penalty kick: A shot is taken on goal as a result of a foul committed by the defensive team in its penalty area or "box." All players except the goalie and the player taking the kick must be outside the penalty area when the kick is taken. Penalty kicks are also called "PKs" or "penalties" and can be used to decide a tied championship game. They are very stressful yet exciting events.

Penalty mark: Also called the penalty spot. A circular mark nine inches in diameter made twelve yards out from the center of the goal where the ball is placed when a penalty kick is to be taken.

Red card: A red card is given to a player who has committed a serious foul or series of bad fouls during a game. A coach or even a parent can also get "red carded" for yelling at the referee or other bad behavior. Anyone who receives a red card must immediately leave the field. If a player receives a red card, her team must continue the game down a player, and she cannot play in the next game.

Shin guards: Protective equipment worn by players to aid in prevention of injuries to the shin.

Shot: An attempt to score on the opponent's goal.

Striker: A position name given to a player in a central attacking position.

Throw-in: When the ball is thrown in by the team that did not kick it out of bounds.

Yellow card: A cautionary measure used by the referee to warn a player not to repeat an offense. A second yellow card in a match results in a red card.

Acknowledgments

Soccer Sisters has been so much fun to write. To me, it's more than just a book series: Soccer Sisters is really about sharing all the love of soccer and friends from a lifetime of playing, coaching, and now, watching as a parent and spectator. I always played soccer because I love the game, love being out on the field, and I hope that is why girls today continue to play. Over time though, I came to see the opportunities I had helped me become the person I am today, and I am grateful to the sport for all it has given me. I also grew to understand the opportunities afforded to me are not the same for girls in other parts of the world. Accordingly, the first thank-you in this book has to go to Caitlin Fisher, founder of the Guerreiras Project (guerreirasproject.org), and Beatriz vaz e Silva, Tayla Caroline Pereira dos Santos, and Adriane dos Santos. These women in Brazil shared their struggles and hopes with me and Brandi, and they inspired me to create the character Flavia. The Guerreiras Project works to use soccer to promote gender justice and support the girls of Brazil to play. I am also grateful to Kely Nascimento-DeLuca for reading the manuscript and educating me further on girls and women in Brazil. Please be sure to see her note at the back of *One on One* to learn more about how we all can support women around the world striving to get the chance to play and better their own lives.

This series would not be possible without the incredible Sourcebooks team. Annie Berger, a patient and thoughtful editor: thank you for making the books so much better. Steve Geck, Sarah Kasman, Alex Yeadon, Katy Lynch, Beth Oleniczak, Elizabeth Boyer, Nicole Hower, and everyone at Jabberwocky who have supported all my crazy ideas, and in particular, for believing in the Play It Forward Project and all it stands for. Shane White, thanks for bringing this book to so many clubs, camps, and leagues. Dominique Raccah, I'm proud to be part of a house led by a woman, supporting women writers and stories for girls. My agent at Aevitas Creative, Lauren Sharp, thank you for believing in the series from the start, and Ed Klaris at Klaris IP for all your guidance.

Thanks to Lucy Truman for the fantastic cover art that really brings the series and the girls to life.

Brandi Chastain, Stacey Vollman Warwick, Marian Smith, and Dan Love, thank you for your support of every part of Soccer Sisters. Nothing happens without a team and you are the best. Chrystian Von Schoettler, your site development and logos are amazing and you are a joy to work with.

As always, I would never be able to write these books without the love of my incredible husband, Diron, and our two kids, Lily and William. I am also very grateful to our large and loving extended family and their unending belief in the series and in me. Verenice Merino, you always inspire us with your love, smarts, and warmth, and you make our lives better every day. Paula Fernades, thank you for making everything so easy. Makena Ward, thank you for letting me use your first name. Your fire and passion for soccer is contagious and inspiring.

I believe that every kid—boy or girl—should have the opportunity to play sports if they want to. The Girls of Armenia Leadership Soccer (GOALS) continues to fight for girls to have equal opportunities in the villages of Armenia. I am grateful for everyone who supports their dreams, especially Zach Theiler, Victoria Dokken, Ed and Alecko Eskandarian, and the entire GOALS team.

Coaches Across Continents, you are changing the lives

of Soccer Sisters all over the world, and it's an honor to call myself a member of your team. Nick Gates, Nora Dooley, Kevin O'Donovan, Adam Burgess, Brian Suskiewicz, Markus, Judith and Bill Gates, and every single person at CAC, thank you for all you do to make the world a better place through sports.

I've also had the great support of many coaches and clubs here at home. Matt Popoli, Jon Feinstein, Luis Arenas, and everyone at NY Surf, thank you for supporting the books and sharing them with your players. Don Cupertino and everyone at Quickstrike FC, I'm grateful for your support with the Play It Forward Project and for believing in Soccer Sisters. Positive Tracks, Soccer Without Borders, Syncitup Soccer, Soccer Girl Probs, the U.S. Soccer Foundation, Grassroots Soccer, Goals for Girls, and so many other fantastic organizations are making soccer a powerful vehicle for change around the world. Thank you for all you do to support girls and sports. Let's keep it going.

Don't miss the first two
books in this great series!

About the Author

Andrea Montalbano is a writer, advocate, coach, and soccer player. She grew up playing soccer in Miami and took that love to Harvard, where she was a cocaptain and a Hall of Famer. She then attended Columbia University's Graduate School of Journalism, kicking off a long career at NBC News as a writer, producer, and supervising producer for NBC News's *TODAY* program. Andrea left broadcast journalism to write books and authored *Breakaway* in 2010. Determined to create a series for girls, she spent the next few years writing the three Soccer Sisters novels. Off the field, Andrea is an activist for using sports for social change and has represented the U.S. government abroad to teach the importance of sports for girls. She is a founder of the Girls of Armenia Leadership Soccer charity and is also on several boards for Coaches Across Continents, a global leader in education through sports. She has enjoyed coaching her own two children on local club teams and lives with them and her husband, Diron Jebejian, outside New York City.